Alexa was crying.

In public. In fr... ...
pregnant and b...
It was terrifyir...

She pulled aw...
disturbingly s...
for a tissue. S...
sternly told her hormones she wouldn't stand for
tears again. When she was certain they'd got the
picture, she downed the rest of her tea, lukewarm
now, because of the tears, and looked at him.

His expression was inscrutable. She didn't know if
that made her feel better or worse. But she couldn't
rely on him to make herself feel better. So she took
a deep breath, held it for a few seconds, then let it
out. It was shaky at best, hitched at worst. She did
it again, and again, until it came smoothly. Then she
said, "I'm pregnant."

Dear Reader,

I suspect I might love drama. At least in the books I write. How else can I explain *Her Twin Baby Secret* to you? It has two rival restaurant owners, a fake relationship, a secret pregnancy and *twins*. I would feel sorry for what I've put Alexa and Benjamin through, except their story has a happy ending. The growth, banter, and lighthearted and emotional moments they experience along the way are merely a bonus. :)

My favorite thing about this book, though, is that I can totally see it as a movie. It's romantic, funny and the perfect break from reality. I hope it'll be something special for you, too! If you'd like to get in touch, you can find me on social media or through my website.

Until then, enjoy Alexa and Benjamin!

Therese

Her Twin Baby Secret

Therese Beharrie

HARLEQUIN®
Romance™

Recycling programs for this product may not exist in your area.

ISBN-13: 978-1-335-55616-5

Her Twin Baby Secret

Copyright © 2020 by Therese Beharrie

This edition published by arrangement with Harlequin Books S.A.

For questions and comments about the quality of this book, please contact us at CustomerService@Harlequin.com.

Harlequin Enterprises ULC
22 Adelaide St. West, 40th Floor
Toronto, Ontario M5H 4E3, Canada
www.Harlequin.com

Printed in U.S.A.

Being an author has always been **Therese Beharrie**'s dream. But it was only when the corporate world loomed during her final year at university that she realized how soon she wanted that dream to become a reality. So she got serious about her writing, and now writes books she wants to see in the world featuring people who look like her for a living. When she's not writing, she's spending time with her husband and dogs in Cape Town, South Africa. She admits that this is a perfect life, and is grateful for it.

Books by Therese Beharrie

Harlequin Romance

Billionaires for Heiresses

Second Chance with Her Billionaire
From Heiress to Mom

Conveniently Wed, Royally Bound

United by Their Royal Baby
Falling for His Convenient Queen

The Tycoon's Reluctant Cinderella
A Marriage Worth Saving
The Millionaire's Redemption
Tempted by the Billionaire Next Door
Surprise Baby, Second Chance
Her Festive Flirtation
Island Fling with the Tycoon

Visit the Author Profile page
at Harlequin.com for more titles.

For Grant, who would pretend to be in a fake relationship with me so I can save face in a heartbeat. If we weren't already married, I mean. I love you.

For the online friends who've become my community. I didn't ever think you could exist, but I'm so grateful you do.

Praise for
Therese Beharrie

"All in all, *From Heiress to Mom* is a delightful, funny, sweet, excellently paced, and very real book. You can tell that a lot of love and care has been put into this book...."

—*Goodreads*

PROLOGUE

ALEXA MOORE HAD never thought the pressure her parents had put on her her entire life would result in this. She barely contained the squeal of excitement tickling her throat.

Her father was sitting beside her in the car, her mother at the back. Both were staring at their phones. They were either checking their emails, replying to emails, or writing their own emails. Leighton and Karla Moore were simple in that way. Work came first; everything else, second. They'd reconciled having a family in light of those priorities by treating their children as though they were work. That was why Alexa and her younger brother by a year, Lee, were raised to function much as their parents did: work was the most important thing. Being Leighton and Karla's children, they had to work harder than anyone else.

Who needed a loving, emotionally supportive family anyway?

But that wasn't for today. Today was for happiness and new beginnings. She wasn't stubborn enough not to acknowledge her parents' contribution to this moment. It was part of why she'd brought them with her. They were the ones who had suggested—instructed—her to start working as soon as she turned sixteen. They'd told her to give them half of what she earned, and because she was their child she'd asked them to help her invest the other half. On her graduation from her Honours degree in business, they'd gifted her with a policy they'd taken out with that money. It had been an impressive nest egg. And it had kept growing while she attended culinary school.

She'd got a bursary to study at Cape Town's Culinary Institute. She was lucky. If she hadn't, she would have had to use that nest egg and she wouldn't be able to move forward with her dream. Her parents had paid for her studies in business on the condition that she got distinctions for all her subjects. She had, though not easily, because she knew she'd already disappointed them by not taking the mathematics bursary an elite tertiary faculty had offered.

But her dream was her dream. A business degree helped her get to that dream—and helped her please her parents more than culinary school had. Their disappointment was worth it for this moment though. She had no student loans, four years of business knowledge, two years of culinary knowledge, and two years' experience in the industry. She was finally ready. This was the last step.

She pulled up in front of the property, letting out a happy sigh before she got out of the car. The brick façade of the building was as appealing as it had been the first time she'd seen it. As the first time it had encouraged her to take a chance on it.

'This is it.'

She clasped her fingers together behind her back to keep from fidgeting.

'This?'

'Yes.' She straightened her spine at the disapproval in her father's voice. 'It's an up-and-coming neighbourhood.'

'It looks unsafe, Lex,' Karla said.

'Oh, it's fine.' She waved a hand. 'You know how Cape Town city centre is. The fanciest road is right next to the dodgiest one. Besides, there are so many people around.'

As if proving it, a group of young people walked past them. They were most likely students; not exactly her target clientele. But everyone had to start somewhere, and students meant lecturers and parents and more mature people who would come to the classy joint in the dingy neighbourhood for the feel of it. She jiggled her shoulders.

'I'm going to call it In the Rough, because this place is a diamond in the rough.' She grinned. 'It's going to be—'

'Lee, darling!'

The world either slowed at her mother's exclamation, or Alexa's heart was pumping alarmingly fast. Why was her brother here? How much of what she'd said had he heard? Would he use it against her?

'What are you doing here?' she asked, her voice cool, a reaction to mitigate the heated emotions those questions had evoked. She would not show them that vulnerability. 'I didn't tell you about this.'

'Dad did,' Lee said, taking their father's hand in a quick shake. 'He told me about a week ago you were planning on showing them a property. Gave me the address and everything, so I could check it out myself.'

'Why would you want to?'

'I can't check on what my big sister is doing with her life?'

No, she wanted to answer. She would have, if their parents weren't there—they would disapprove. Somehow, after years of trying and failing to obtain their approval, she still wanted it. After years of her brother using that desire as a weapon to compete with her, she was still offering it to him.

'To be fair, I'm not doing this with my life yet.' She was trying to be civil, like she always did. Because she was still trying to be a decent person with Lee, too. When would she learn her lesson when it came to her family? 'I wanted Mom and Dad to see this place before I put in an offer.'

'I know.'

'Did you want to see it, too?'

'Oh, I already have.'

She frowned. 'Why?'

'Because I made an offer.' He shoved his hands into his pockets, his smile catlike. 'The owner accepted it this morning. This place is going to be mine.'

There was a stunned silence. Her parents broke it by asking Lee why he'd bought the place. Bits and pieces of his answer floated across to her. He wanted to secure the place as a surprise for Alexa. It was a smart business decision to invest in property, particularly in a neighbourhood that was fast becoming one to watch. If he and Alexa worked together, there was less chance of failure. The Moores could become a powerhouse in the hospitality industry.

Lies. Lies, all of it.

Lee spoke to them as fluently as he did his other languages. His linguistic skills were as impressive as her mathematical skills. He knew five of South Africa's eleven official languages; he also knew how to fool their parents. They thought he was a good, supportive brother when in reality, he was a master manipulator. All for the sake of winning a competition he'd made up in his head where they were the only competitors and he the only willing participant.

'Alexa,' Karla called. 'You're daydreaming, darling.'

She blinked. 'Sorry.'

'Did you hear what your brother did?'

'Yes.'

'Aren't you glad?'

'Why would I be glad?'

Her mother exchanged a look with her father. Leighton took the baton.

'Lee's made the smart decision here. It's not a buyer's market at the moment, so you might not have got the property. He has more capital, and more clout, so he had a better chance of being successful in the purchase.'

'He didn't know about the property before you told him,' she said numbly. 'And he only has more capital because he's been working longer.' In the business sector, which was more lucrative. Even her nest egg couldn't beat that. 'The owner said she hadn't had much interest in the six months the property's been on the market.'

'She did sound thrilled with my offer.'

She turned at the satisfaction in Lee's voice. When she saw it reflected on his face, her heart broke. This didn't feel like the other times. When he'd race to the dinner table, turn back to her and say, 'I win!' though he'd been the only one running. Or when he would bring a test home from school, announcing that he'd beat Alexa's mark from the year before.

This was more malicious. It was…uglier. And it proved that she would always be a target Lee would shoot at, no matter what the cost.

Unless she did something about it.

'I hope you find a tenant soon, Lee.'

'Wait!' he said when she started walking to her car. 'I thought you'd rent it?'

'So you can pop in whenever you want? Make your presence known in my business? Pull the rug out from under me when I think I'm safe?' She shook her head. 'I appreciate the offer, but you'll have to find someone else.'

'Alexa, you're being foolish.'

'No, Dad, I'm being realistic. But this is a great neighbourhood.' Her voice cracked, echoing her heart. 'He'll find someone to rent from him soon enough.'

'Darling, your brother only wants to help.'

She took a deep breath before offering her mother a smile. 'I know.' Even after he'd punctured a hole in her dreams and her parents were defending him, she couldn't be blunt. 'I can't take his help or I wouldn't be making the Moore name proud, would I? It's all about achieving things we can be proud of. I can't be proud of this.'

Another breath.

'You should go to the restaurant I booked for us tonight with Lee. He deserves it.' She smiled at her family, well aware that it didn't reach her eyes. 'I hope you enjoy the food.'

She got into her car and drove away, leaving her heart and her dreams shattered behind her.

CHAPTER ONE

Four years later

'OH,' ALEXA SAID FLATLY. 'It's you.'

Benjamin Foster couldn't help the laugh that rumbled in his chest. 'Yes, it's me.'

Alexa Moore, owner of the elite Infinity restaurant, and the woman who probably hated him more than anyone else in the world, glowered.

'You need to stop following me.'

'I'm not following you,' he denied.

'Are you sure? You seem to be everywhere I am.'

'Because we're in the same business.'

Her eyes stopped scanning the room and settled on him. Sharpened. 'You're here to offer Cherise de Bruyn a job.'

He tilted his head. 'How did you know?'

'You think I didn't hear about Victor Fourie being poached from In the Rough?' She smiled, but it wasn't friendly. 'It's terrible when karma does her thing, isn't it?'

'I'm not sure why she would get involved.'

She gave him a look. He allowed himself a small smile.

'Fine, I do know.' A few seconds passed. Something cleared in his brain. 'You're here to offer Cherise a job, too.'

She responded by ignoring him. He shouldn't have wanted to smile. It seemed rude to since he was the reason she had to offer Cherise a job. She hadn't confirmed that was why she was there, but he was fairly certain. When the thought of being rude did nothing to deter his amusement—apparently what his presence did to her tickled his funny bone—he turned to the barperson and ordered a drink.

'Can I get you one?'

'I don't want to owe you one, so no, thank you.'

He *tsk*ed. 'That's not very mature, Alexa.'

'Maturity is for the weak,' she muttered under her breath.

He didn't bother hiding his grin this time, but paid for his drink before he replied. 'I don't agree with that.'

'Why would you, Benjamin?' she said with a sigh. 'I said it. On principle, you can't agree with me lest *you* seem weak.'

'"*Lest*"?'

'It means to avoid the risk of.'

'I know what it means. I'm wondering why you said it.'

She sighed again, as though he were chopping up the last of her patience. Which was probably true. They'd known one another for eight years now. Or perhaps it would be better to say they'd known about one another for eight years. They didn't know one another, not by a long shot. They had only gone to the Culinary Institute together, the current venue of their meeting, and met on and off in the six years after that.

Whenever they did, they rubbed each other up the wrong way. It caused a friction so intense that sometimes Benjamin struggled to figure out how he felt about her. On the one hand, she never backed down, said interesting things like *lest*, and made him laugh. On the other hand, she was his greatest competition.

Who could be friendly with the competition?

Infinity was rated highly on all the important websites. He often heard whispers of the patrons of his own restaurant comparing In the Rough's food or ambience to Infinity's. It wasn't uncommon for patrons to do so; comments like that were part of the business. But her restaurant was the one he heard mentioned most frequently. It was also the one they preferred most frequently.

'Really?' she asked when he leaned against the bar. 'In this spacious, beautiful, but most importantly *spacious* place, you couldn't find someone else to bother?'

'Bothering you is more fun.'

Her reply came in the form of a glare. He smiled back, sipped from his drink, and didn't move. He did watch though.

She was right—the venue was gorgeous. It was nestled in the valley of one of the many vineyards in Stellenbosch. Bright green fields stretched out in front of them courtesy of an all-glass wall. The room they were in, usually a dining hall, had been transformed for the sake of the graduation. Chairs were set out in rows, a small stage had been erected on one side, and the opposite side housed the bar they were at. On the other side of the glass wall, accessed through a door on the side, were tables and chairs under tall trees.

He remembered sitting there many a lunch time when he'd been at the Institute. Hell, he remembered watching Alexa glower at him from inside the dining hall much in the same way she was doing now. He'd known even then that she was dangerous. How, he wasn't sure.

'What the hell is he doing here?'

The words weren't meant for him, but he heard them. When he followed her gaze, he saw the cause. Her brother, his business partner, was there. Benjamin didn't know why. Securing a head chef was more in line with Benjamin's responsibilities. But their partnership had evolved in the last four years, and their roles weren't what they initially were when they started working together.

Back then, Benjamin was the head chef and

Lee's management company dealt with the running of the restaurant. Benjamin had since taken over some of those responsibilities, which was hard to do without a head chef. It meant that Benjamin's time was still needed in the kitchen. For three glorious months after Victor Fourie had been persuaded to work for In the Rough, Benjamin had been able to explore more of the management side of things. As it turned out, he enjoyed running a restaurant more than spending all his time in the kitchen.

But Lee had been acting strangely when it came to this head chef thing. With Victor Fourie, Lee had actively encouraged Benjamin to go after the man even though he knew Victor worked for Alexa. It had started out harmlessly enough. They'd been out for drinks one night, discussing work, when the chef walked into the bar. It had seemed like a perfectly fair move to ask him to join them. After that night, Lee had told him to get Victor to take over some of Benjamin's responsibilities. Since it would take an immense amount of pressure off Benjamin, he'd done it, though he hadn't understood Lee's insistence. Now Lee was here…

'Ben!' Lee said when he saw them. His eyes flickered to his sister. Something Benjamin didn't like shimmered there. 'Fancy seeing you here.'

'Is it?' Benjamin asked, taking Lee's hand. 'I told you I was coming.'

'He has to pretend it's a surprise in front of me,' Alexa said, her voice emotionless.

He'd only ever heard her speak that way with her brother. He would have thought, after his and Alexa's antagonistic history, she would have aimed that tone at him, too. But when she spoke to him, her voice was icy, or annoyed, or full of emotion, none of which he could read. He found he preferred it.

'If he doesn't,' she continued, 'it would be clear that he's really here because of me.'

'Not everything I do is because of you, Alexa.' Lee said it smoothly, but Benjamin could feel the resentment.

'I wish that were true.'

Lee didn't acknowledge that Alexa had spoken. 'What I am surprised about is finding you two together.'

'Why?' Benjamin asked.

'Don't you hate one another?'

He looked at Alexa; Alexa looked at him. For a beat, they said nothing. Her expression changed then, going from icy cool to warm. His heart thundered in response to her hazel eyes opening. They grew lighter when they did, so that he could see the green flecks in the light brown. In a way no grown man should experience, Benjamin's knees went weak.

Her eyebrow quirked, as if she knew, though there was no possible way she could. But the show of sassiness pulled the side of her face higher, softening a defined cheekbone. It was an extraordinary juxtaposition to the other side of her face, which was untouched by the expression. It was still hard lines and sharp angles. That had never applied to her lips though, one side of which was now quirked up—much like her brow—in amusement. At him. He was amusing her.

Because he was admiring her full lips that looked as soft as dough. An interesting comparison, though not surprising since he regularly dealt with dough. What *was* surprising was that he wanted to mould that dough as he did in the kitchen. But with his lips instead of his hands, though he could imagine brushing a thumb over those soft creases…

He took a long drag from his drink, severely disappointed that it wasn't alcohol. He could have done with the shock, the burn of downing a whiskey. But no, he'd decided he shouldn't drink because he wanted a clear head when he spoke to Cherise.

How was this clear?

'Well, Lee,' Alexa said, her voice as smooth as the brandy he'd longed for. Or had he thought of whiskey? 'You know what they say: hate and love are two sides of the same coin.'

Lee's head dropped. 'What are you saying?'

'You don't know?' She turned to Benjamin. 'You kept your word. How lovely of you.'

Benjamin didn't know what was going on, but he understood he shouldn't say anything.

'There's no way you and Ben are dating.'

'You're entitled to believe what you want to, Lee. We don't owe you explanations.'

'You're dating her?' Lee asked Benjamin now. 'No. Of course not. You would have told me.'

'I asked him not to. Apparently his loyalties are divided now.' She wrinkled her nose. 'I shouldn't have said that. It was insensitive.'

She grabbed Benjamin's hand. Good thing he was still numb from shock, or he might have felt that explosion of warmth from the contact.

'I'm sorry, Ben.'

Their eyes met again. Nothing he could read on her face gave him any clues to her feelings. No plea that he play along; no acknowledgement that this was strange. Or maybe there were clues, but he couldn't recognise them.

Then she smiled at him. Her mouth widened, revealing strikingly straight white teeth. Those lips curved up, softening all the lines and angles of her face. Even her gaze warmed, though he had no idea why or how. It was a genuine smile that both stunned and enthralled him. He couldn't look away.

'Oh, you *are* together.' Lee's voice penetrated the fog in his brain. 'Wow. I can already see the headline in *Cape Town Culinary*: "Rival restaurant owners fall in love".' He paused. 'Maybe we should get the photographer to take a picture of you two now for the article? I'll call her over.'

Both of them wrenched their gazes away from one another to stare at Lee.

CHAPTER TWO

Lee shifted with unease and when she recoiled from the shock, she set the water she'd been churning on the boil. *Stop that snort,* she told herself. *I think she's been stupid to me mind.*

She looked at Emilio or them... for the most part, looking beyond the many... that she had to admit he'd... when she'd heard her when he'd... Though now, of course, she was on something that he was her son again. She'd done been a deep one... she'd not care so... what about the debate she... about women the world now, of course, as some... as that... as of the way she'd told me that she was being and it would reach at him...

CHAPTER TWO

'I'D RATHER NOT,' Alexa said when she recovered
from the shock. She set the water she'd been
drinking on the bar, slid off the stool. 'If you'll
excuse me, I think some fresh air would do me
good.'

She looked at neither of them. Not the man
who'd broken her heart too many times for her to
count; not the man who'd helped her brother do it.
Though now, of course, she was pretending that he
was her boyfriend. She alone, because Benjamin
had not once said a word about the elaborate tale
she'd woven. He would now, of course. As soon
as she was out of the way, he'd tell Lee that she
was lying and they'd laugh at her.

Nausea welled up inside her. She hoped it didn't
mean she'd throw up. She could already imagine
Lee's questions: *Rough night last night, sis? Or
are you pregnant?* He would laugh, she wouldn't,
and he'd know something was up. The last thing
she needed was her brother discovering her secret.

She soothed the panic the idea evoked by reminding herself that Lee's presence in the last four years had generally made her queasy. That could be the answer now, too. The thought calmed her. Remembering she'd been feeling surprisingly good these last months helped, too. She took a breath, exhaled slowly. She was one week away from entering her second trimester. Once she got there, she'd tell her parents, and there would be no chance Lee could tell them for her.

It might have been a little paranoid—but then, it might not. She had a brother who was intent on ruining her life after all. Telling their parents she was pregnant before she could was exactly the kind of thing he'd do. She wouldn't get the chance to tell them the story she'd practised since she'd decided to do something about her need for a family. Not the broken one she currently had, but a whole one. A safe one. A family she could actually trust.

As usual, the thought sent vibrations through her. Pain, disappointment prickled her skin. She stopped walking, bracing herself against a tree as she caught the breath her emotions stole. She didn't get the chance to.

'You haven't seen me in months and this is how you treat me?'

She closed her eyes, put all her defences in place, and turned. 'I thought you'd get the message.'

'What message?'

'I don't want to see you, Lee,' she told him. 'I don't want you in my life.'

Something almost imperceptible passed over his face. 'We're family. You have no choice.'

'I'm aware that we're family.' She took a deep breath. 'That's the only reason we've seen one another at all in the last four years. Mom and Dad have birthdays, and there are special days, like Christmas and…' She broke off. She didn't have to explain anything to him. 'Anyway, we have to see one another at those occasions. But not outside of them.'

'All this because I bought a building you wanted?'

'You know it wasn't only a building,' she snapped. Pulled it back. But it was hard to contain. It sat in her chest like a swarm of angry bees, waiting to be let out. She could *not* let it out. 'You've insisted on making this about you and me, but really it's about you. It's always been. I want to live my life without you. You can't seem to live yours without me.'

He smirked. 'You're putting an awful lot of importance on yourself.'

'No, you are.'

She meant to stride past him, but his hand caught her wrist.

'I assume you're here for a new head chef. What happens if you don't get one, Lex?' he asked softly. 'You can't keep running Infinity and its kitchen.

You must be spreading yourself thin since your last chef left.'

'He didn't leave. You stole him. You and Benjamin stole him.'

'Which makes me wonder how your romance bloomed?' Lee's lips curved into a smile that broke her heart. Because it was mean, and so unlike that of the brother she'd once thought she had. 'Were you looking for revenge? Maybe you thought you could make him fall in love with you, then break his heart? Or maybe use your body to—'

'Lee.'

The voice was deep with unbridled emotion. Both she and Lee looked in the direction it came from. Benjamin stood there, watching them with a glower she'd never seen on him before. He was usually effortlessly charming, which had been one of the reasons she didn't like him. No one could be that charming, certainly not *effortlessly*. Her conclusion had been that he was a demon, or some kind of magical being sent there to test her patience. The test was going smoothly. Her results were not as positive.

His disapproval should have been aimed at her then, considering their history of battling against one another. But it wasn't. It was aimed at Lee. A thrill went through her before she stomped it down viciously. She did a few more jumps on it for good measure.

'Ben,' Lee said with a smile. He tended to reserve the vicious side of his temperament for her. 'Didn't see you there.'

'I thought as much. I doubt you'd be talking to Alexa that way if you did.'

Benjamin's eyes met hers. She wasn't sure how she knew it, but he was asking her if she was okay. She angled her head. He looked back at Lee.

'You should probably get someone to help you if that's your perception of relationships.' He held a hand out to her. It took her a moment to realise he meant for her to take it. As if someone else were in her body, she did. 'Even so, I have to say I'm not thrilled with your implication. Alexa and I are in a healthy relationship. Neither of us is using the other. Unless there's something you want to tell me, Lex?'

Oh. He was keeping the pretence going.

Oh.

She shook her head.

'If I say something corny like "I'm using you for your addictive kisses", would you be mad?' he asked.

There it was, that effortless charm. It was kind of nice when it was being used for good. To help her instead of annoy her.

'You probably shouldn't say it, to be safe.'

He laughed. For a moment, it was just the two of them, amused at one another. A part of her wiggled with glee; another part told her to take a step back. This was confusing, and happening too fast. She wasn't even sure what 'this' was.

'Seriously?' Genuine confusion lit Lee's face. 'I thought this, you two, were a joke.'

'You were accusing Alexa of those things earlier and you thought this was a joke?' Benjamin's voice had switched from charm to ice.

Alexa cleared her throat. She didn't want this turning into a full-on brawl. Even if the prospect of seeing Lee punched brought her more joy than it should have. She was strangely certain that would be the outcome if she didn't intervene.

'Ben and I agreed to keep business and our personal lives separate,' she told Lee. 'That's why no one knew about our relationship until today.'

'And you told *me*?' Lee asked. 'Now I know you two are lying.'

'You don't have to believe us, Lee.'

But she really wanted him to. Maybe that was why she went along with what Benjamin said next.

'He doesn't have to believe us, but why don't we show him why he should?'

When he looked at her, asked her permission with his eyes, she nodded. Told herself wanting to make Lee believe her was why she'd went along with what Benjamin did next. But all of that dissipated when he kissed her.

* * *

He'd never wanted to punch someone as much as he'd wanted to punch his business partner in the last few minutes. He wasn't sure if it was because Lee was acting almost unrecognisably, or if his instincts were tingling because he *did* recognise the way Lee was acting. It was the same way people in his past had acted. They'd need something from him, then act surprised, attacked, victimised when he asked them if they were taking advantage of his desire to help.

His instincts could also have been tingling because despite his past, he still wanted to help someone who needed him. It was clear Alexa did. It was his weakness, helping people. Not when the help was appreciated; only when the help was taken advantage of. He didn't know where Alexa fitted into that. It didn't keep him from kissing her though.

Not his best decision, though his lips disagreed. They heartily approved of the softness of Alexa's lips pressed against them. She smelled of something sweet and light; reminded him of walking through a garden at the beginning of spring. It felt as though he'd been drawn into that scene when her mouth began to move against his. His body felt lighter, as it often did after a long, dull winter and the sun made its comeback. He could easily imagine the two of them in that garden, surrounded by flowers, overcome with the joy and happiness a new season tended to bring.

The taste of her brought him sharply back into his body.

He hadn't intended on *really* kissing her. A quick meeting of lips was enough to convince her brother they were together—people who didn't like one another didn't kiss at all. He assumed. Before he started to kiss this woman he supposedly didn't like.

There was no time to think of it since his tongue had somehow disobeyed his desire to keep things simple. Instead, it had slipped between Alexa's lips, plunging them both into complicated.

But damn, if complicated didn't feel *good*. She was sweet, spicy, exactly as her personality dictated. The tangling of their tongues sent pulses through his body, settling in places that made him both uncomfortable and desperate. He used it as an excuse to rest a hand on the small of her back, pressing her against him. She gave a little gasp into his mouth as her body moulded against his, but she didn't pull away. She did the opposite in fact, reaching her arms around his neck and pulling herself higher so their bodies were aligned at a more pleasurable height.

It was that thought that had him pulling away. He wouldn't embarrass himself in public. More importantly, he couldn't embarrass Alexa. Both would happen if they didn't pull themselves together.

She didn't protest, lowering herself to her feet

again, her gaze avoiding his. But then she shook her head and looked at him. Curiosity and desire were fierce in her expression, but it was the confusion that did him in.

Was it brought on by this little charade they were performing? Or was she surprised at the intensity of their kisses?

'Happy?' she asked.

He almost answered before he realised she wasn't talking to him. Good thing his brain had started working in time. He would have said something he couldn't take back if he answered. Something in the vicinity of a *yes and no* and maybe a few other statements.

Lee was watching them with a frown.

'You two really are together.'

'So you keep saying.'

'I mean it this time,' Lee said. His next words were directed at Benjamin. 'You've complicated things.'

No kidding. 'You didn't know about us for months.' *Because there was nothing to know.* 'We'll be fine.'

'I'm sure Cherise de Bruyn agrees.'

Benjamin thought that was a strange thing to say until he saw the jerk of Lee's head to the side. Cherise stood with her fellow graduates, watching the three of them with a bemused smile on her face. Considering he'd spoken to her first thing when he arrived, he was sure Alexa had, too. Now Cherise was watching the two people competing for her to work for them kiss, and was probably wondering what the hell would happen next.

To be fair, so was he.

CHAPTER THREE

ALEXA PAUSED AT her front door, wondering why she was doing what she was doing. No answer she came up with made her feel better about doing it, so she simply unlocked the door. She stepped aside to let Benjamin pass her, then closed it and resisted—barely—leaning her forehead against it. Alexa couldn't give in to her impulses any more. They were what had got her into trouble in the first place. If she hadn't pretended Benjamin was her boyfriend, she wouldn't be letting him into her home now to discuss the way forward.

It seemed particularly cruel that she had to do that here. Her home was *her* space. It was where she recovered from long, rough days. It was where she cried when the pressure of running a business got to her. It was where she remembered her complicated feelings when her sous chef had brought in her new baby.

Kenya had come in to show the baby around and had brought her mother, too. There had been so much love between the three of them. Alexa had watched it, her heart breaking and filling at the same time. When Kenya had handed her the child, that breaking stopped. She'd remembered all those times she'd thought family couldn't only mean competition and neglect. She hadn't seen examples otherwise, but she'd hoped. Then, between her studies, work, and her brother ruining her dreams, she'd forgotten that hope. Until she'd seen Kenya and her family. Until she'd held that baby.

She'd remembered that, once upon a time, her dreams had included having a family. A warm, happy family with people who loved and respected one another. She thought about how she had no one to go home to at night. How the idea of dating and trusting someone so she could have someone to go home to made her feel ill. A new idea had popped into her head then. One year later, whoops, she was pregnant and there was no going back.

It wasn't so much *whoops* as going through vigorous fertility treatments and being artificially inseminated twice. But *whoops* was what she planned to tell her parents. Rather their disappointment that she hadn't been careful than tell them she didn't want anyone in her life who could hurt her the way they had.

She was clearly in a very healthy mental space.

'Nice place,' Benjamin said, breaking into her thoughts.

'Thanks.'

It was more invasive than she'd anticipated, having him look at her stuff. But they needed privacy, her place was the closest, and it was better to be here than at Infinity. There was more of her there, and with their baggage, it had felt wrong to take him there.

It wasn't that she wasn't proud of her home. Everything in it had been put there for a reason. The beige sofas were comfortable and expensive, the first items she'd bought for the flat. The restaurant had still been a baby, so it had taken most of her disposable income to buy them. She had slept on them for four months. They weren't as comfortable as a bed, but then, she hadn't been sleeping much anyway. She had been fuelled by the desire to succeed, and three to four hours of sleep were more than enough in those days.

The coffee table had come next, then the dining room set, both made from the most gorgeous stained wood. The fluffy carpet had been an indulgence considering she still hadn't had a bed, but filling the open-plan lounge and dining-room had been more important to her. It had made the flat feel like a home.

Her priorities had then shifted to her bedroom, which took her six months to complete. Last was her kitchen, separated from the dining room by half-wall, half-glass, with an opening on the right. The style somehow managed to give the impression of being open-plan, but offered privacy, too. She hadn't had the money to do what she wanted in the kitchen for the longest time, which was why she'd left it for last. Besides, she had everything she wanted at her restaurant, and that was enough.

After a year and a half, her kitchen was exactly what she had imagined it would be. Her appliances were top-of-the-range. Shelves were strategically placed all over the room; spices near the stove, fresh herbs near the window. Cupboards were filled with the best quality ingredients, and close to where they were needed. She'd added colour with fake plants, because her energy was mostly focused on keeping the herbs alive and there was too much competition for the light. And her utensils! Those were colourful, too, though pastel, which made her feel classy and grown-up. Heaven only knew why.

'I didn't expect it to be quite this...warm.'

She threw her handbag onto the sofa, shrugged off her coat. 'Because I'm so cold-hearted, you mean?'

'Not at all.'

'Then what did you mean?'

'It's just...' He looked around, as if to confirm what he was about to say. 'It really is lovely. Everything fits. It's like you selected each thing on purpose.'

'You didn't?' she asked. 'In your own home?'

'I don't have my own home.'

'What do you mean?'

'I live with my parents.'

She stared at him. She didn't know how long it was until his lip curled.

'You have an opinion on that?'

'No,' she replied. 'I don't.'

'You have an opinion on everything. Also, your face is saying something different.'

'You're right. I do have an opinion. But I don't want to share it.'

It was pure stubbornness, since sharing her opinion would have been the perfect segue into the questions she had. Why was he, a successful adult, still living with his parents? She knew he was successful because In the Rough was her main rival, according to reviews and social media, and she was pretty damn successful, despite the forces working against her.

It still smarted that they were succeeding with a restaurant that had been meant to be hers. The location, the property, the name—Lee had stolen it all from her. Then he'd gone and recruited Benjamin to work with him. Lee could have chosen *anyone* else. Actually, she was sure that Lee had specifically chosen Benjamin because the man annoyed her so much, though she wasn't sure how Lee would know that. Either way, Benjamin annoyed her more now that he was in cahoots with her brother. At least before, he'd annoyed her on his own merits.

He'd singled her out their first day at the Institute. She had no idea why, since she minded her own business. For some inexplicable reason, he'd decided she was partly *his* business, and he began to compete with her. She'd instantly recoiled; she had enough competition in life. She hadn't cut Lee out of her life and minimised her contact with her parents, only to replace them with a negligible man-child.

Now she had to work with the man-child.

'Would you like some alcohol?' she asked after a deep sigh.

His eyes flickered with amusement, contrasting the tighter lines on his face. 'Anything you want to give me is fine.'

She bit her tongue before she could reply. She hadn't thought of anything to reply with, but her tongue was often quicker than her brain. She didn't want to take the chance of saying something inappropriate. Such as how what she wanted to give him was another kiss to see if the spark she'd felt was a fluke...

She poured him a generous glass of whiskey from a bottle that was still three quarters full and settled on water and peppermint for herself.

'You're not having any?' he asked, accepting the glass from her.

She leaned back against the counter on the opposite side of the kitchen. 'I'm on an alcohol fast.'

'Why?'

She rolled her eyes. 'Does it matter?'

'You're annoyed because I asked?'

'Yes, actually. It's rude.'

Plus she didn't have a good answer for him. She hadn't anticipated him asking why she was fasting from alcohol. She should have known he wouldn't be polite and leave it at that though.

'Sorry.' His lips twitched. 'So...'

He didn't say anything more. She didn't speak either. The silence stretched between them like a cat in the sun. Then, as a cat would, it stared Alexa in the eyes, unblinking, until she sighed.

'This is what dating you is like?' She didn't wait for an answer. 'How disturbing.'

How she knew exactly what to say to get under his skin was what was really disturbing.

But then, disturbing seemed to be the theme of the night. What with the fake relationship, the kiss, being in Alexa's home. He'd offended her by noting that her flat was homey, but he couldn't help but be honest. She'd done an amazing job turning what would have been a trendy, but not particularly special place into something he could imagine coming home to.

Well, not him, exactly. He had his own home. With his parents. Which she had an opinion on, but wouldn't tell him about because she was stubborn. He couldn't be upset by it since he was stubborn, too. If she'd asked why he still lived with his parents he wouldn't have told her.

Not that any of it was important now.

'Cherise saw us.'

'I know.' She drained her glass. Her gaze rested on his, before it rose to his face. Something about it made his body feel more aware. 'Would you like some more?'

He glanced at the glass. Empty. Strange. He didn't remember drinking from it. Except for that one time when he'd taken a long, deep gulp and—

Ah, yes. He remembered now.

'No, thank you.' Probably best with all the disturbing stuff happening.

'Tea, then? I'm making myself some.'

'Anything to avoid having a straight conversation with me?'

'What is this we're having, then?' she asked, filling the kettle with water. She took out two mugs, despite the fact that he hadn't answered her. 'A skew conversation? Diagonal?'

'Funny lady.'

Amusement flickered in her eyes. 'I try.'

'To annoy me, yes,' he muttered.

The amused light danced in her eyes again. He felt an answering light in his chest. He didn't care for it. It made him think the tables had turned.

'I know we have to talk about this.' She took out ginger from the fridge, sliced up some pieces and threw it in one cup. She looked over at him. 'Tea? Coffee?'

'Coffee. Please,' he added as an afterthought.

She began to make his coffee, expression pensive. 'I suppose I wanted to make the conversation easier. Less awkward. A discussion over hot drinks seemed like something that would help with that.'

His mother would like her, he thought before he could stop himself. Usually, he was more careful when it came to comparisons between his mother and people he wasn't related to. Hell, people he was related to, too. It tended to evoke protective feelings in him when he did. He blamed it on the fact that he felt protective of his mother, so when he recognised something akin to her in someone else, those feelings bled over. It had too often in the past, and he'd been hurt because of it. Which should have made him more careful. It usually did. Except now, apparently.

'How did I manage to upset you with that?' she asked, more resigned than curious.

'You didn't.' A lie. Or half-lie. He'd upset himself, but because of something she'd said.

Her eyes narrowed, but she finished his coffee, slid it over the counter towards him. She finished her own drink with a teaspoon of honey, then leaned back against the counter as she had with her water.

'Okay, so let's talk straight.' She bit her lip, then

straightened her shoulders. 'I'm sorry for pretending you're my boyfriend. It was an impulse.'

'Why did you?'

She tilted her head, as if considering his question. Or perhaps considering whether she'd answer it.

'My brother is a jerk.'

He stared.

'You can't possibly not have noticed,' she replied at the look. 'He's entitled, and competitive, and generally unkind. I wanted to push him off a cliff. Since literally doing so would send me to prison, I settled for figuratively. You were the figurative.'

He took a minute to process that.

'He's normally a decent guy.'

'Maybe to you. But since you said normally, I think you recognised that he wasn't decent today.' She paused, her lips pursing. 'He normally isn't decent with me.'

Lee's behaviour today didn't encourage him to disagree with her. So he didn't.

'It's weird that you pretended *I* was your boyfriend. You hate me.'

'You were the closest person,' she said coolly, not denying his statement. 'Also, you're his business partner. Best cliff.' She shrugged.

He took a steadying breath. He didn't like being used. He'd had too many instances of it in his life. His last girlfriend, his father's colleague, his cousin. Those were but a few, but they were the most recent. Remembering them had him steeling himself against Alexa's charm—or whatever it was that kept him standing there.

'I don't like being used.'

'I'm sorry.' Her voice and expression were sincere. 'I'm sorry for putting you in a position to be used. For using you.'

It was that sincerity that had him saying, 'Apology accepted,' when he wasn't entirely sure he meant it.

'Thank you.' There was a brief pause. 'So maybe now you can explain why you decided to go along with the charade. Maybe you can apologise for that kiss, too.'

CHAPTER FOUR

The expression on his face was comical. But, since she'd asked him a serious question, one she would very much have liked an answer for, she decided not to give in to the smile. To wait.

His expression became more comical. His mouth contracted and expanded, as if he were mouthing what he wanted to say, but not quite. Emotions danced in his eyes, though she couldn't put her finger on what they were. But really, it was that tick near his nose, which she'd never before seen, that amused her the most.

Still, she didn't smile.

'I thought… I mean, he was… I wanted to…'

His stammers made resisting the smile harder. It was strange. She had never before spoken with him long enough to have to resist any of her emotions. Usually, those emotions ranged from irritated to downright angry. Amusement generally didn't feature; not unless it was tainted with satisfaction. This wasn't. This was simply… amusement.

An alarm went off in her head.

'You wanted to *what*?' she asked, her words sharp, marching to that alarm.

He cleared his throat and met her eyes. His expression was now serious.

'I wanted Lee to stop acting like a jerk.'

'Well.' It was all she said for a while. 'You succeeded, just for a moment.'

'But at what cost?'

His eyes bored into hers, and her face began to heat. Was he asking how she'd felt about that kiss? If he was, he'd have his answer in her blush.

Because it had embarrassed her, she assured herself. Her fingers lifted and slipped under the neckline of her dress. She lifted it, let it fall, sending air down her body, which had suddenly become clammy. For some reason, her skin was itchy, too. It was exactly how she felt on a summer's day in the kitchen. Hot and sticky, but satisfied at what she was cooking up.

Wait—satisfied? Where had that come from? What was happening to her?

Embarrassment, an inner voice offered again. She clung to it. Ignored the fact that her memories of that kiss, of how she'd felt much as she did now while he'd been kissing her, were vehemently disagreeing.

She took a deliberate sip of her tea. She'd put enough ginger in it that the flavour burned her throat. She relished it. Then met his eyes.

'A high cost,' she told him. 'It means Cherise thinks we're dating.'

He was watching her closely. She hoped to heaven he hadn't developed the ability to see into her head. 'And now she's confused about our opposing offers.'

'I tried to tell her the same thing we told Lee,' she said with a sigh. 'The whole "we're dating, but we're keeping our personal and professional lives separate" thing. I don't know if she bought it. She's certainly confused by it.'

'Me, too, to be honest with you.'

He gestured, asking if she'd like to have a seat in the lounge. She would have, desperately, since her body was aching from a day of standing. Her baby apparently didn't like that kind of strenuous activity. But it felt too intimate, sitting with him on the sofas she'd bought and slept on for months. A twinge in her back urged her to reconsider, and she spent hopelessly too long trying to decide. In the end, she strode past him without answering, as though it had been her idea all along.

Man, pregnancy was making her *stubborn*.

It was definitely the pregnancy. She didn't possess a stubborn bone in her body normally.

She sank into the sofa as soon as she sat down, a sigh leaving her lips immediately. His brows were raised when she looked at him.

'Why didn't you say something?'

'About what?'

'Needing to sit down.'

'I didn't need to.'

'So what you did now wasn't you finally relaxing and your body thanking you for it?'

'I have no idea what you're talking about.'

He shook his head, but the sides of his mouth were quirked. 'Stubborn isn't an appealing quality.'

'I don't care if you find me appealing.' She didn't give herself a chance to figure out why that felt like a lie. 'Besides, it's been a long day.'

'You get stubborn after a long day?'

'That's what I said, yes.'

'Is it because you're tired?' He was outright smiling now. Taunting her, really. 'Or is it a physical symptom? Aching legs, sore back, stubborn personality?'

'Yes.' It wasn't an answer, but it was all he'd get. 'Now—what are we going to do about Cherise?'

The smile faded, but the twinkle in his eyes didn't. He was sitting beneath the light fixture, which could account for that twinkle. But it didn't; she'd seen that twinkle before. It appeared whenever he was amused with her. It was frustrating to know. More frustrating was how attractive that amusement made him.

It danced in his brown eyes, crinkled the skin around them. That forced his cheeks up, which spread his full lips—lips she now knew had objectively impressive skills. None of that factored into how the angles of his face were affected. Warming them, softening them; perhaps a combination of the two. Either way, it dimmed his arrogance, that self-assured *I know I'm successful and handsome* edge of his. That edge was as devastating as it was irritating, particularly as it always seemed to be directed at her.

'What were you planning on doing about Cherise before all this happened?'

She snorted. 'Wouldn't you like to know?'

'Yes,' he deadpanned. 'That's why I asked.'

'You asked so you could outdo whatever I planned to do.'

'I wouldn't dream of it.'

'Like you wouldn't dream of stealing my head chef? Who was already working for me, I might add. Happily. For months.'

'That can't be true if he left,' Benjamin pointed out softly. 'It didn't take me much to convince him either.'

'Are you defending *stealing* my chef?'

'I didn't steal him. I…gave him another option.'

'You stole him,' she said flatly. 'Probably at the behest of my brother, because, as I mentioned before, he's a jerk.'

He hesitated, which gave her the answer. And disappointed her, strangely. Why, she wasn't sure. It might have been because he'd defended her in front of her brother and hadn't freaked out completely when she'd pretended he was her boyfriend. But one day's experience couldn't erase years of experience to the contrary. That experience had taught her that Benjamin Foster could be just as much of a jerk as her brother.

'I think you're on the right track though,' she powered on. If she did, it would help get him out of her house and she'd finally be able to rest. 'We do what we intended to do and let her make the decision as she would have without this complication.'

'We're not continuing the charade?'

She thought about it. 'We have two options, I suppose. One is that we do, but only verbally. If she asks, we'll talk about one another lovingly. Affectionately. Then, in a few months, we break up.'

'And the other option?'

'Tell her the truth. We were playing a joke on Lee.'

He went quiet for a few seconds. 'But if Lee finds out, we both look foolish. We'll have to answer why we were so…' he hesitated '…*invested* in proving we were together.'

'There's that,' she said slowly. She didn't want him to know she'd thought about that, too. Not to mention she hated the idea of Lee discovering the truth. He'd take such pleasure in it. He'd probably hold it over her head every time she'd have the misfortune of seeing him. 'There's also the implication that we're friends. Why would we play a joke on Lee if we weren't?'

'You're worried about people thinking we're friends, but not that we're in a relationship?'

'Well, yeah. At least there's a physical aspect to a relationship. People would think I was distracted from your personality because you look the way you do.'

He frowned. She could almost see his brain malfunctioning. Mostly because she was pretty sure that was what was happening to hers.

'Is that a compliment?'

'No,' she answered immediately.

But it was. She couldn't figure out why she'd said it.

She vowed there and then never to admit she found him attractive again. She wouldn't even *think* about his broad shoulders and full lips. He certainly wouldn't kiss her again either, so she'd have no reason to. And if she did think it—and he did kiss her—she'd remind herself there were high stakes involved.

She laid a hand on her belly, feeling the slight curve. At this stage it could have been a good, generous meal as much as a baby, which amused her. She stroked her thumb over the curve, mentally assuring her child that she'd protect it. She paused when she saw him watching her.

What was it about being in his presence that made her lower her guard?

She moved her hand.

'Fine. We'll pretend to be together,' he said

curtly. 'But only because Lee deserves to think it, after how he treated you.' He paused, as though something had just occurred to him. The frown deepened. He was scowling when he continued. 'We'll do whatever we intended to do with Cherise. I'll keep talk of our relationship with your brother to the minimum. We should both do that, to whoever we meet.' He downed the rest of his coffee and set the cup on the table. Stood. 'And in a few months, our fake relationship will end. It'll be as clean as this situation allows.'

'Er...yeah, sure.'

She set her own mug down, confused by the change in his temperament. But that was the least of her problems. She'd just realised her pregnancy wouldn't be a secret for much longer. People would have questions about the paternity of her baby. If she said it was Benjamin, she would be dragging him down an even more convoluted path. If she said it was some random guy as she'd planned to, people would do the calculations and accuse her of cheating on Benjamin.

Oh, no.

She really should have thought about this earlier.

'Benjamin, I think we need to talk about—'

'We've talked about everything already, haven't we?' he interrupted. His eyes were sharp, and she almost shivered from the intensity of them. So she just nodded.

'Great, then we don't have to see one another again for a while.'

'Okay.' Numbly, she followed him to the door.

'Thanks for the drinks.'

'Okay.'

'Good luck with Cherise.'

'Thanks.'

And then he was gone, leaving her to think about the extent of the mess she'd created that day.

The resolution he and Alexa had come to regarding their fake relationship went up in flames the moment he walked into In the Rough the next morning.

'You're dating my sister?' Lee asked, sitting arms folded at a stool in front of the bar. Apparently, he'd been waiting. 'What the hell, man? Do you have no boundaries?'

It wasn't early in the morning. In the Rough only opened from lunchtime, so generally he worked from home for a couple of hours when he woke up, then made his way to the restaurant at about nine. His staff would start trickling in then, too, most of them there by ten, and then it would be a bustle of activity until they closed at eleven at night. This morning, he'd been particularly grateful for the quiet so he could figure out what the hell had happened the night before.

One moment he'd been deciding whether to let

Alexa's backhanded compliment slide, the next he was watching her stroke her stomach and his gut had clenched with need. It made no sense, but that gesture had seemed somewhat protective. It reminded him of the times he'd seen pregnant women do the same thing. Though Alexa probably wasn't pregnant, it had made him think about a life he'd never wanted. He was too busy taking care of his parents to even consider it.

Not that he minded; not in the least. His mother was lovely. Sharp and charming and the kind of mother who made sacrifices for her children. Except there were no children, only him. And that sharpness and charm and kindness didn't negate the strain of her illness.

They'd had no idea what caused it for a long time. His mother had been his father's admin help at the panel-beaters' company his father owned and ran. For ten years, almost, until she'd started complaining about the pain right after she'd had Benjamin. Aches that felt like they were all over, restricting her movement, making simple tasks hard to carry out. Doctors had prescribed ibuprofen, diagnosed her with the flu, told her she'd strained a muscle, or pushed too hard, or that she needed to take a break.

But even when she took a break, the pain would continue. Sometimes, if she stayed in bed and rested, it would make it worse. The doctors maintained they could find nothing wrong. It was the eighth doctor she'd gone to in four years who had diagnosed her with fibromyalgia.

His life hadn't changed dramatically, or at all, with that diagnosis. His father had simply sat him down and explained as best he could to a four-year-old that his mom was sick. Frank Foster had told Benjamin to try not to bother his mother as much when she was in bed. Maybe Benjamin could even help out a little more at home. He hadn't known the difference between that and what he'd done before, except now it came with the weight of verbal responsibility.

But she was his mother, and he wanted her to be happy. As he grew older, he thought having him couldn't have helped with his mom's pain. Because she'd made sacrifices for him at the cost of her own health, physical and mental, he would do the same for her. So he had. For the past twenty-odd years he had helped his parents. Now he cared for his parents. There wasn't really room for him to consider caring for anyone else in that situation either.

That pulse of need he'd felt with Alexa the night before? A fluke. There was nothing more to it. And he didn't engage with it any more because something more significant had occurred to him when he'd been talking with Alexa.

Now might be the time to confirm it.

'Did you hear me?' Lee demanded.

But maybe not before he'd had another cup of coffee.

'Mia,' he said to the tall woman behind the counter. 'Is the machine on?'

'You know it,' she replied with a sympathetic grin. It made him realise she'd heard what Lee had said. 'The usual?'

He unclenched his jaw slowly. 'No. Double espresso, please.' Her brows lifted, but she only nodded. He looked at Lee. 'Can you wait for me in the office? I'll be there in a second.'

'Mia, could you please add another cappuccino to that?' Lee said. 'And bring it to Ben's office when it's ready?' He shook his head. 'Or have someone else bring it. Sorry. It slipped my mind.'

Her smile didn't waver, but something on Mia's face tightened. It probably wasn't because Lee had been referring to her disability—the limp that Benjamin hadn't once asked about because it was none of his business—but because Lee had done so poorly. Benjamin wouldn't have expected it from him; Lee handled most things smoothly. Then again, he hadn't expected Lee to be a jerk to his own sister, so maybe he didn't know his business partner as well as he thought.

'Yeah, sure,' Mia said.

'Thank you.'

Lee gestured for Benjamin to lead the way. After one last glance at Mia to make sure she was okay, Benjamin walked away from the enticing smell of coffee to his office. It was a simple room. Not very big, but there was enough space for his desk and cabinet, and the large windows gave it an airy feel. Unfortunately, those windows looked out onto a car park with a busy Cape Town road just behind it. But that was the price he paid to be in a central location.

At least, that was what Lee had told him when he'd been courting Benjamin. Over the years, Benjamin had begun to believe him. Was he a fool to do so?

'This isn't your only business,' Benjamin noted, taking off his jacket and slinging it over the chair. 'Surely you have better things to do than to wait for me to talk about something that isn't business.'

'Except this affects our business,' Lee said with none of the charm, the ease Benjamin had once been privy to. 'Honestly, Ben. There are millions of women in South Africa, but you decide to sleep with my sister?'

'Watch it,' Benjamin growled, though he had no reason to defend Alexa. Apart from their fictional relationship. Which was not, as the title stated, real.

'She's already changed you,' Lee replied with a shake of his head. 'You weren't foolish before yesterday. Hell, the last time we spoke, you knew how important getting Cherise de Bruyn to work with us was. But now you're letting your head be messed around by your—'

'Be careful about what you say next.'

Lee's jaw tightened. 'This isn't going to work.'

'What isn't?' he asked coolly, leaning back in his chair. 'This partnership? Or my relationship with your sister?'

Lee opened and closed his mouth several times before he said, 'The relationship.'

'That hardly seems like any of your business.'

'It's literally my business.'

'No, my relationship has nothing to do with this business.' He paused when one of his waiters brought in their coffees. 'Alexa and I have been able to keep our relationship under wraps for months. It hasn't affected the way I've run things around here.'

'And yet here you are, snapping at me.'

'Because for some reason, when it comes to your sister, you change, too, Lee.' He downed the espresso. When it seared his stomach, he remembered he'd forgotten to eat breakfast. 'I don't like the way you treat her. I don't like the way you treat me when it comes to her.'

It was a warning.

'I thought this wouldn't happen.'

'What does that mean?'

'I thought working with someone who competed with my sister meant *I'd* be working with someone who competed with my sister.'

And there it was. Confirmation of his suspicions. When he told Alexa he wanted to continue the charade because of how Lee treated her, he realised there was more to it. It was because of how Lee had treated him, too. Lee had used him. Much as so many other people in his life had.

'My relationship with your sister doesn't have to affect the way we do things around here,' he said coldly. 'It won't for me. I'm perfectly capable of working with you and dating your sister. Since you two don't have a relationship, it shouldn't matter to you anyway.'

Lee's face was tight. Benjamin couldn't read what caused that tightness, or what was behind it. All he could see was a complicated mess of emotions. Since he had enough of those himself, especially after Lee's little bombshell, he didn't need to figure Lee's feelings out.

'We won't let your involvement with my sister affect the business.'

Benjamin gave a tight nod.

'What about our friendship?'

Benjamin didn't know how to answer that. He didn't trust Lee any more. How could they still be friends?

'See?' Lee said. 'You're already treating me differently.'

'I've explained why.'

He'd use Lee's treatment of Alexa as the scapegoat here. He was sure she wouldn't mind. They were in this together after all.

Lee exhaled harshly. 'Fine. We'll just pretend you're not dating my sister.'

'What?'

His mother stood in the doorway, eyes impossibly wide.

'You're dating Benjamin Foster?'

Alexa's feet stopped working. That meant she was standing in the doorway of her office, frozen by both the words and the stare of accusation from Kenya.

'Who told you that?'

'You should have.'

'How did you find out?'

'A friend of mine was at Cherise's graduation yesterday.' Kenya leaned back in Alexa's chair. 'She asked me why I didn't tell her. Apparently, you and Benjamin were hot and heavy yesterday and it was the talk of everyone there. *And I didn't know.*'

'It hasn't been going on for very long,' she grumbled. *Like, less than twenty-four hours.* 'Besides, I didn't want people to know. It's new.'

And fake.

'Am I still people, Alexa?'

The question was serious enough to make Alexa blink. When she recovered from the shock, Kenya was watching her, waiting for an answer.

'I… I didn't tell anyone.'

Kenya stood, nodding slowly as she did. 'Yeah, why would you tell anyone? Least of all someone you've worked with for four years. Least of all someone who considers you a friend. Clearly that doesn't apply to how you consider me, does it?'

It would be so easy to get through this. If Alexa told Kenya the relationship was fake, contrived when she'd been desperate and in a panic to get away from her brother, Kenya wouldn't be upset with her.

She opened her mouth, but nothing came out. Not a single word.

What would happen if she told Kenya the truth? She'd look like a fool, for one. But Kenya might tell her friend, who might tell their friend, and before she knew it both her and Benjamin's reputations would be ruined. Not to mention that her brother would find out. And she couldn't face Lee's smirk when he heard she'd made up the entire thing for his sake.

'You can't even dispute it,' Kenya said, hurt thick in her voice. She strode past Alexa. Alexa wanted to say something, but her phone rang before she could. Picking up the landline, she barked, 'Yes?'

'Benjamin Foster's on the line for you,' came the voice of one of her waiters.

She bit back a sigh. 'Put him through.'

'Alexa?'

His deep voice was even more disturbing over the phone. Now she had to imagine his face. And for some reason it came without the arrogance that usually put her off.

'You called for me, didn't you?'

'Yes, I did, darling.'

'Darling? Really?' She looked behind her to ensure no one was there. 'You realise we're on the phone, right? No one else can hear what we're saying.'

'I'm here with my mother.'

'Your mother?'

'She'd like to meet you.'

'She'd like to… Wait, I'm missing something, aren't I?'

'Yes.'

It was the first time she felt as though he was answering her properly.

'Are you free for dinner tonight?'

'I'm not, actually. I'm working. As are you, considering we run restaurants.'

'I'm sure you can take an evening off for this *very important date.*'

She rolled her eyes. Belatedly, she realised he couldn't see her. She let the disappointment pass through her.

'Look, Benjamin, I don't know what's going on, but there's no way I'm going to meet your mother.'

'She would like to meet you.'

She could hear he was clenching his teeth.

'Is she giving you a hard time, Benny? Let me talk to her.' There was a short pause where Alexa could swear she heard Benjamin apologise. 'Alexa? This is Nina, Benjamin's mother.'

She closed her eyes. 'Hi, Nina.'

'Is it possible for us to meet?'

'Mrs Foster.' Alexa cleared her throat. 'I, um, I'm not sure.'

'Be sure, dear.' There was admonishment there, but Mrs Foster spoke again so quickly Alexa barely had time to process it. 'This evening might be too soon, considering your commitments. How about tomorrow evening? Could you arrange for someone to take care of things then?'

'I…um… I…don't know…'

'I just wouldn't want to meet you at your restaurant, dear.' Mrs Foster gave a sparkling laugh. 'You'd have to come out and speak to me in front of your employees and… Well, I don't need to tell you how awkward that might end up being.'

'No,' Alexa said numbly. 'You don't.'

'So it's settled, then! I'll see you tomorrow.'

'I… Yes, you will.' She cleared her throat. 'Could you please put Benjamin back on the phone?'

'Of course.'

There was another pause, then a, 'Yeah.'

'I have an hour for lunch today and clearly we

need to talk. Can you meet me at St George's Mall at one?'

'Yes.'

'It wasn't a real question, but I'm glad you agreed. It makes things easier.'

CHAPTER FIVE

'WHAT WERE YOU *THINKING*?'

It was the first thing Alexa said when she saw him. A bit rude, in his opinion, but he allowed it because she'd made a good impression on his mother. Nina had murmured her approval and patted his cheek in affection. All this came after she'd read him the Riot Act for keeping his relationship a secret.

'Hello, Alexa,' he said calmly. 'Would you like to have a seat at one of the coffee shops? It is lunch, after all. And I haven't had breakfast. A busy morning,' he added, taking her elbow lightly and steering her through the crowds of people milling about. 'What with speaking to your brother about our fake relationship, having my mother find out about it, and then, of course, my actual business, which is open, but why would they need the manager and acting head chef there for the lunchtime rush?'

'I have responsibilities, too.'

'And yet here we are, gallivanting in the middle of the day.'

'It's not gallivanting.'

But she said it under her breath. He took it as agreement. How could he not?

St George's Mall had once been a busy street in Cape Town, but it had been reimagined for pedestrians. Now people walked through the bricked area lined with green trees and yellow umbrellas without the bother of traffic. There were three men playing drums a little way away from them, a boy who couldn't be older than nine dancing to the beat. Tourists browsed through the stands selling jewellery and African-inspired crafts. Residents walked with purpose to get to where they needed to be, or stopped at one of the cafes to grab something to eat. Police presence was heavy, but quaint, since they monitored the area on horses.

It was one of his favourite places, just fifteen minutes away from his restaurant. It screamed with the vibrancy of Cape Town, which was one reason he loved his city. He wasn't sure why Alexa had suggested it, since it was further away for her than for him. Could she have been considering him? Or was she merely trying to minimise the chances of someone she knew seeing them together?

He would have related to that, except his mother already knew, so his father would, too, and they were the main people he cared about. It was too late for keeping secrets for him.

'Hey,' she said, snapping her fingers. 'Can we sit here? Or should I ask another time?'

'Sorry,' he muttered, and gestured for her to sit.

They took a few minutes to look at the menu. At least, he did. She'd glanced at hers quickly, then set it down and was now watching him.

'You must be thinking it's a pity you don't have X-ray vision with how you're staring at me.'

'Hadn't considered it before, actually. Just like I hadn't considered having to talk to your mother and be manoeuvred—quite expertly, I might add—into having dinner with your family.' She slapped her hand against her leg under the table. *I'm not even your girlfriend.*

He exhaled, hoping the nervous energy in his body would escape from his lungs. No such luck. It stayed in his chest, bouncing around as though it were being chased by a happy puppy.

'Let's get something to drink.'

'Why would you let your mother think we're in a relationship?' she asked, ignoring him. 'This turns something that could easily be solved into something so much more—'

'Alexa,' he interrupted, his voice slicing through her panic. 'Let's get something to drink. We can talk about it afterwards.'

Her jaw locked, but she nodded. The waiter came over. He ordered sparkling water—he needed a break from the coffee. It was probably the cause of the nervous energy. Probably—and Alexa got rooibos tea. When the waiter left, Alexa stared wordlessly at him. To emphasise her displeasure, she folded her arms and leaned back.

He took a deep breath.

'My mother being under the impression we're together wasn't my fault,' he said slowly. 'Lee ambushed me this morning—' that was more aggressive than what Lee had done; or maybe not '—and when he was talking about the relationship, my mother walked in. I'd forgotten some papers at home and she thought I might need them.'

He could hardly be upset with her for being sweet.

'Anyway, she found out, and since I've never told her about any of my relationships, she kind of latched on to the information. I couldn't tell her it was a lie without…' He grasped on to the first thing he could think of. 'Without your brother overhearing it.'

'Couldn't you have told her when he left?'

'No.' Anger made the word choppy. 'She was excited. I couldn't disappoint her.'

'People survive disappointing their parents.'

The words were so unexpected, so cool, his anger fizzled.

'Is that what happened to you?'

'It doesn't matter.' Her features softened, but the lines around her mouth were still tense. 'What's going to happen when she finds out we're not really together, Benjamin? You don't think she's going to be disappointed then? You don't think she's going to hate knowing that you lied to her? That you don't have a girlfriend?' She blushed. 'I mean, I'm assuming. I don't care about your romantic—'

'Of course I don't have a girlfriend,' he said, affronted. 'Do you think I'd be pretending to be your boyfriend if I did? Do you think so poorly of me?'

She stilled, though her eyes, big and bright, remained steady. 'You want me to say no, but experience has taught me I can't say that without reservation.'

He had no reply to that. What could he say? But it left a bitter taste in his mouth that she thought that of him. He didn't deserve it. The only thing he'd done that was morally ambiguous was offer her chef a job at In the Rough. Even then he'd done things above board. Victor Fourie had accepted Benjamin's offer without a comment about what he'd left behind. In the same way he'd left In the Rough behind when he'd moved on a couple of months ago.

Then again, he could see why she'd have that opinion of him. He worked with her brother, a man she had no relationship with. A man who treated her poorly, and apparently went out of his way to do so. Lee had used Benjamin to that end, too, and he'd unwittingly become a tool to hurt

Alexa with. Frankly, he was still working out how he felt about it. Especially since he'd considered Lee a friend until all this had happened.

His fake relationship had thrown everything into upheaval. Including his relationship with his mother. He wasn't proud of it, but he couldn't bear to break his mother's heart. Up until today, he hadn't even known his mother wanted him to be in a relationship. But the happiness in her voice as she questioned him about his girlfriend—his first, according to her—told him otherwise.

He couldn't tell her it was all fake. He loved her too much. And yeah, maybe he'd get over disappointing her. But in that moment, it hadn't even occurred to him.

The waiter interrupted his thoughts, and when the man walked away, he sighed.

'I'm sorry. About my mother. I wasn't thinking. Or I wasn't thinking properly.'

She held the mug in her hands as if to warm herself, though it was a typical summer's day.

'I've been there,' she murmured. Then she set the mug down and took her head in her hands instead. 'I was there—yesterday. Because of my stupid brother, I caused this mess and—'

She hiccupped. An actual hiccup that was most likely the precursor to a sob. His hand shot out of its own volition, grasping her arm and squeezing in comfort. A hand left her head and rested on his hand.

And just like that, he knew he was in trouble.

Of course, he'd known that before. The entire thing with Alexa was, as she said, a mess. But before, he'd still had some control over his actions. He wasn't helping her because she needed help. Well, not *only* because she needed help. He also wanted to help her with his own free will. The moment she showed him vulnerability, though, that free will had waved goodbye and jumped on the nearest plane to anywhere but his mind. Because now he wanted to help her because she *really* needed help. She was distraught, and things needed to be fixed, and he was the ultimate help when things needed to be fixed.

He'd done it with his mother and father for most of his life, more so as an adult. He'd done it with his last girlfriend. His cousins. Friends. And he would do it now, with Alexa.

He curled his free hand into a fist.

She was *crying*. In public. In front of him. Because she was pregnant and because she had to tell him the truth. It was terrifying.

She pulled away from his touch, comforting— disturbingly so—as it was, and reached into her bag for a tissue. She found one, mopped herself up, and sternly told her hormones she wouldn't stand for tears again. When she was certain they'd got the picture, she downed the rest of her tea, lukewarm now, because of the tears, and looked at him.

His expression was inscrutable. She didn't know if that made her feel better or worse. But she couldn't rely on him to make herself feel better. So she took a deep breath, held it for a few seconds, then let it out. It was shaky at best; hitched at worse. She did it again, and again, until it came smoothly. Then she said, 'I'm pregnant.'

He stared at her.

She cleared her throat. 'So, you see, you have to tell your mother the truth or she'll think the baby's yours and things will get more complicated.'

He still stared at her.

'I wouldn't have told you if I didn't have to. I went over it in my head a million times last night, and again, after that phone call with your mother.'

He didn't say a word. She pursed her lips when they started to shake.

No, she told the tears that were threatening. *I had you under control. You can't disobey me.*

'I didn't want you to know,' she said, thinking that speaking would distract her. 'I didn't want *anyone* to know until I had no choice but to tell them. No one knows besides you. Because somehow, my decision is now going to reflect on you.'

He kept staring, but his mouth had opened. She had to wait a while longer before he said anything.

'You're pregnant?'

She nodded.

'We have to tell people the truth.'

She clenched her teeth when the statement brought a fresh wave of heat to her eyes. She would *not* cry in front of him. Not again.

'Okay.' Her voice broke as she said it. Damn it.

'They'll think the baby's mine, Alexa,' Benjamin said, his voice pleading. 'My mother and your brother and everyone else. We can't just break up then.'

'Why not?' she asked desperately. 'Who cares what they think?'

'I do.' His face was stern. 'It'll be my reputation on the line.'

'It doesn't have to be,' she said, desperation once again taking the wheel. 'You can tell them I cheated on you.'

'*What?*'

'Make me the bad guy.' She hated the thought of it, but it was her only option.

'You'd rather have everyone think you cheated than tell the truth?'

'I don't care what everyone thinks,' she said heatedly. 'If Lee finds out I made this up because of him...' She met his gaze. 'He took my property and my restaurant years ago and he had no reason to. If I give him this, it'll fuel him for years.'

'What do you mean, your property? Your *restaurant*?'

She scoffed. 'Please don't pretend you don't know what Lee did. It's an insult to you and me both.'

'I have no idea what you're talking about.'

He seemed genuinely confused. Though that could have as easily come from the news that she was pregnant as from this. She sighed.

'I found the building for In the Rough. Came up with the name, too, because of the neighbourhood. I was determined to turn that place—*my* place—into a diamond.' The memory of it curved her lips. 'I went through hundreds of listings to find it, and I was so excited because it was *finally* time. I'd spent eight years working towards that moment, and finally...' She trailed off when a wave of sadness crashed over her. 'Anyway, I was supposed to take my parents to see it. I mean, I did take my parents to see it. But I made the mistake of telling them where it was when I scheduled the event with them a week before. We always had to make plans in advance with them.'

She shook off the resentment that she'd had to schedule the meeting with her parents in the first place. Second, but not by much, was that they'd told Lee.

'They told Lee, and he bought it out from under me. He offered to rent it to me. I declined. He would have never allowed me to do what I wanted to do.' She waved a hand. She wasn't sure what it was meant to signify. 'And then I heard you two had become partners. It made sense. If my brother was the devil, I suppose I considered you a demon. My dreams had turned into my own personal hell.'

It was as funny as it was heartbreaking. She was sure the small smile she hadn't been able to resist conveyed both.

'I knew none of that.'

'Would it have changed anything if you had?' she asked, wanting to know.

A complicated array of emotions danced across his face. She supposed she could understand it. It was a good business decision to be a partner with Lee. He came with property, a smart name, business knowledge, and experience. He also came with baggage: her. She had no idea whether Benjamin cared about that, but what she'd told him now didn't reflect well on Lee regardless. Unless he shared Lee's opinion of her, and her brother's lack of scruples, in which case it wouldn't change anything.

But he wouldn't look this tortured if things hadn't changed for him, would he? Or was she grasping at straws, desperate for someone, anyone, to finally be on her side instead of Lee's?

'It's smart to be in business with Lee,' came the careful answer. 'He's a good businessperson.'

'You still think so after what I told you?'

The stare flickered. 'He's been good to me.'

She licked her bottom lip before drawing it

between her teeth. Then she nodded. 'I suppose that's fair.'

Disappointing, but fair. But it helped sharpen her idea of him. She'd been faltering on what she thought of him because he hadn't deliberately set out to hurt her with the restaurant. But after what had happened with her chef, and now, with his opinion of Lee remaining unchanged... It was best if she didn't think he was someone he wasn't.

'If we tell my brother the truth, he'll use it against you, too,' she said.

His lips parted, as if he hadn't considered it. Or maybe he didn't believe it was possible.

'It's too complicated to continue this lie, Alexa.'

She exhaled. 'Okay.' It was time to leave. She needed to recover from all this in private. She needed to prepare, too. 'Give me a few days. It shouldn't make a difference for you, but it'll help me figure some things out.'

He gave a slow nod. 'Then I guess I'll tell my mother.'

'Let me.' She had no idea why she said it, but it was too late to take it back. 'I'll come to dinner tomorrow. I'll tell her I dragged you into this and that you were being the perfect gentleman. I'll explain to her what happened with my brother, and how you couldn't come clean with him near by. We'll make you come out of this smelling of roses.'

'Why?'

'It's the least I can do after the trouble I caused.' She took out money and tossed it on the table. 'Call Infinity with the details about tomorrow.'

She hoped he couldn't see her shaking as she walked away.

CHAPTER SIX

HE OFFERED TO pick up Alexa at her flat. Partly because his mother had taught him to be a gentleman, and partly because he felt bad about the way things had gone the day before. He blamed it on his shock. She was *pregnant*, and he was the only person who knew. It seemed significant. It shouldn't have. She hadn't told him because she wanted him to know, but because it made their lie infinitely more complicated. Though he wanted to help her, he couldn't see how to. And he'd disappointed her because of it. But rather her than his mother.

Nina's reaction to the news that he was in a relationship had been surprising. After her shock and the millions of questions that had come with it, she told him how happy she was that he was dating.

'You're always taking care of us, Benny,' she'd said. 'I was worried it stopped you from living your life. But now you have someone!' She had clasped her hands in glee. 'I can't tell you how much I've wanted this to happen.'

He could only imagine how she'd react if she thought he was having a baby. He was worried enough about telling her the truth.

He took a shaky breath and rang Alexa's doorbell. Tried to keep his jaw from dropping when she opened the door almost immediately.

She wore a light pink dress, cinched below her breasts and falling softly over her stomach. He thought it might be a wrap-around dress considering how the material crossed over her body, parting in a slight V at her legs, ending in two different lengths. The V revealed two gorgeous legs, toned, sliding down into heels that matched the exact shade of the dress. There was another V, though he kept himself from looking at that too closely, since it appeared at her chest.

He *had* looked closely enough to notice that her breasts had become fuller with pregnancy.

Not that he had anything to compare them to. He hadn't looked at her breasts before. He'd simply...noticed they were there. She was an attractive woman, and, since he was attracted to attractive women, he'd noticed. And now he noticed that her breasts were fuller. It was all scientific. There was nothing more to it.

He noticed the style of her dress was somehow both highlighting her pregnancy and hiding it. Or did he only think that now because he knew she was pregnant? She wasn't showing apart from the fuller breasts and the slightest curve of her stomach. The dress flattered her body shape, which even before pregnancy had been a glorious mixture of full curves and lean muscle.

She'd always dressed for her body. Sometimes in dresses that made her look demure and saintly; other times in skirts and shirts that made him think she wanted to torment every person in the room around her. Though this dress seemed to fit with her general style—flattering, understated, seductive—at the same time it somehow didn't. It was warmer, softer, though he'd bite his own tongue off before admitting it.

'Are you going to say hello or keep staring?'

He instantly blinked, as if his body was trying to tell her he wasn't staring. But that was undermined by the blush he could feel heating his face. It got hotter when he realised he hadn't looked at her face since she opened the door. If he had, he wouldn't have spent such a long time contemplating her dress or her style, but trying to get his breath back.

She'd left her hair loose. He couldn't remember ever seeing it that way before. It was long, wavy, flowing past her shoulders and stopping halfway to her elbows. She'd parted it so that most of the thick locks had settled on the right side of her face. The rich brown of it bled into the lighter brown of her skin, as if folding dark chocolate into milk chocolate for a deliciously sinful dessert. Just at the beginning stages, before they mixed and created a brown that was more like his own skin tone.

Her lips were painted the same colour as her dress, her checks dusted with some of that colour, too. Her eyes, which were watching him speculatively, were somehow more pronounced, more emotive than usual. He guessed that also had something to do with make-up.

'Keep staring, then,' she answered for him. 'Okay.' She reached behind the door to somewhere he couldn't see, bringing a coat back, which she handed to him. 'Could you at least make yourself useful, please?'

He took the coat without a word, stepping back when she closed the door behind her. Then she looked at him.

'Honestly, Benjamin, this is an overreaction, surely.'

'No.'

'No, it's not an overreaction?' she asked. He nodded. 'You've seen me dressed up before. Mixers at the Institute. Graduation. Ours and Cherise's.'

'Not like this.'

'This is because I'm pregnant and I didn't feel good in anything else.' She straightened her shoulders. 'I know it's probably more formal than tonight required. It's just… The shop assistant told me it suited me.' She lifted a shoulder, though it wasn't as careless as he was sure she intended. It was defensive. 'I thought the dress deserved more effort from other parts of me.'

'Your hair's loose.'

'It has been before.'

'I've never seen it loose before.'

She frowned. 'Well, it's not my preference.'

'I know. That's wearing your hair in a bun.'

'I... Yes.'

She lifted a hand, tucked some hair behind her ear.

'A ponytail would probably be your next option.'

Her lips parted.

'Either on top of your head, when you're working, or at your nape, when you're dressing up.' He had no idea why he was doing this. It felt as if he was seducing her. But surely seduction couldn't happen without him intending it? He kept talking. 'Sometimes you plait your hair in two, then twirl the plaits around your head and pin them like a crown.'

Breath shuddered from between her lips. He swore he heard her swallow. Then she said, 'Only in the kitchen.'

He lifted a hand, pausing before he could do what he wanted. 'Can I touch it?'

'Can you...? My hair?' she asked, her eyes dipping to where his hand hovered above the strands on her shoulder. He nodded. 'Okay.'

'You're sure?'

'Yes.'

She sounded annoyed that he'd clarified. It made him smile. So did the strands of her hair, which were curly and soft and just a little wet.

'I like it like this.'

'In that case, I'll wear it this way more often,' she said dryly. 'It's incredibly practical for someone who owns a restaurant.'

He laughed. Gave in to the urge to tuck her hair behind her ear as he'd seen her do earlier. 'I wouldn't say no.'

She exhaled. 'What are you doing, Benjamin?'

He dropped his hand, looked at her face. 'I don't know.'

'You do know.'

'No, I don't.' He smiled. Almost as soon as he did, the smile vanished. 'Except for right now. Right now, I'm contemplating how to get you to kiss me again. I'd say it's an appropriate response to how incredible you look.' He shook his head. 'I was staring earlier because I didn't have anything to say. You're so beautiful. And so is this dress…and your hair, your face…' He shook his head again. Offered her a wry, possibly apologetic smile. 'I'm sorry. I think the last couple of days have officially caught up with me.'

Her expression was unreadable, but she said, 'It's been a rough couple of days.'

'Yeah.'

'Because of me.' She paused. 'I'm sorry.'

'You don't have to apologise. You already have, anyway.'

'Right.' She leaned back against her door, which he realised only now she hadn't moved away from. 'This hasn't been easy for me either.'

'I know.'

'A large part of it is because you get on my nerves. A lot,' she added when he frowned.

'That seems uncalled for, considering I just gave you a bunch of compliments.'

'You want acknowledgement for that?'

'A thank you would be nice,' he muttered.

'You're right.'

'Sorry—could you say that again?' He patted his pocket, looking for his phone. 'I want to record it for posterity.'

'This, for example, is extremely annoying. But at the same time, I can't stop thinking about the kiss we had the other day.'

He stilled.

'Which gets on my nerves, too. An interesting conundrum. Am I annoyed because I'm attracted to you? Am I annoyed because you annoy me but I'm still attracted to you?' She exhaled. It sounded frustrated. 'I don't have answers, but I keep asking these questions. Then, of course, you do something decent, like pretend to be my boyfriend even though you have no reason or incentive to. You stand up for me in front of my brother, which I found disturbingly hot. In the same breath, you

act stupidly, and tell your mother—your *mother*—
that I'm your girlfriend. Which, tonight, we have
to rectify.'

She shook her head.

'Honestly, Benjamin, these last few days have
been the most frustratingly complicated of my
life, and I'm an entrepreneur with a crappy family. And I'm *pregnant*, about to become a single
mother. Complicated is the air I breathe. But you
make things…' She trailed off with a little laugh.
'And still, I want to kiss you, too.'

It took him an embarrassingly long time to process everything she said. By the time he got to the
end of it, the part where she wanted to kiss him,
his jaw dropped. Trying to maintain his dignity,
he shook his head.

'I don't need someone to kiss me out of charity.
Especially not someone who thinks I'm annoying.' The more he spoke, the more indignant he
felt. 'I'm only annoying because you're annoyed
with everyone. Don't deny it,' he said when she
opened her mouth. 'It was like that at the Institute. You had so many people trying to be your
friend and you'd brush them aside. Draw into
yourself. It's like no one was ever good enough
for you.'

She tilted her head, the muscles in her jaw
tightening and relaxing, one eyebrow raised.
'You're upset—and lashing out—because I called
you annoying?'

'I'm not…' He clenched his teeth. 'This is exactly what I'm talking about.'

'Oh—was this you trying to be my friend? Is this me drawing into myself?'

'You know what?' he said, shrugging his shoulders in an attempt to shrug off the irritation. 'I don't need to do this.'

'No, you don't,' she agreed. 'You should have just kissed me like I asked you to and neither of us would be annoyed now.'

'When did you ask me to kiss you?'

She narrowed her eyes. 'You think I told you I've been thinking about our kiss for the fun of it? That I'm attracted to you because I was ranting?' She snorted. 'You spend an eternity staring at me, telling me you're trying to get me to kiss you, and when I give you permission—'

'That was *not* permission.'

'Yes, it was. I said, and I quote—'

'Shut up.'

'Excuse me?'

'You gave me permission?'

'I did. But if you think you can—'

This time, he shut her up by kissing her.

Apparently, he did think he could. And she wasn't mad about it.

Not about the way his lips pressed against hers with a force that had her pushing back against her front door. Not about the fact that they'd had a ridiculous argument that culminated in this kiss in the passageway of her flat. She had no idea what her neighbours thought. She liked the idea of them cheering her on. It wasn't what she'd be doing if someone was arguing near her flat, but she was uptight like that. Her neighbours generally seemed cool.

None of that mattered now, of course. Benjamin had teased her lips open—it hadn't taken much cajoling—and now their tongues were entwined, moving around one another like two loose strands of a rope longing to be tied. She blamed the inelegance of it on the passion. Their argument had fuelled it, though she suspected it was always there between them, simply because of who they were. She couldn't fault it when it created a hunger that could be sated like this. With his lips moving against her, allowing gooseflesh to take the place of her skin. With his tongue, sending heat to places in her body that had been cool for longer than she could remember.

As if he had heard her, Benjamin's hands began to move. They'd been on her waist, keeping her in place, she suspected. But now they skimmed the sides of her breasts, running along her neck, angling her head so he could kiss her more deeply. The throaty moan that he got in response was a soundtrack for his journey back down, although now he lingered exactly where she needed him to. His touch was gentle at her waist, his thumbs brushing her belly. She gasped. It was intimate, him touching her stomach like that. It felt as if he was claiming her. Her baby.

And that was more intense than when he reached her hips and pulled her against him, bringing the most aching part of her to where she needed him.

But that wasn't true any more. The most aching part of her was her heart now, his innocent caress of her stomach awakening things that she'd forced to sleep years ago. When he pulled back, she offered him a small smile of reassurance. It was okay, him kissing her. She was okay. She wasn't being threatened by the loneliness that always followed her. She wasn't overcome by the enormity of her decision to have a baby alone.

After the thing with Kenya and her baby had happened, Alexa had thought more seriously about having her own. She'd done so with her head *and* her heart. Her head had told her that she was thirty years old, and her ability to become a mother wouldn't always be as simple as it was now. It told her that her business was steady enough for her to take maternity leave, and that when she came back she'd be stronger for having had her baby. If her business took a knock, she was still only thirty, and she'd work her tail off— with even more incentive than usual—to make sure it was back on track.

Her heart had told her that she was ready. She'd

spent her entire life examining what she shouldn't be as a mother; who she shouldn't be as a parent. She was ready to finally have the family of her dreams. Where support, love, inclusion were the norm. She wouldn't push her child to breaking point, or create an environment where her child felt they needed to compete for her love. No, she would create warmth and happiness. A home, as she'd done with her flat.

But that was before she'd lost her head chef. Now her business didn't seem nearly as stable as it had been before. And that was before this kiss with Benjamin. Suddenly she was thinking about whether she was robbing her child of having someone else to love them. If she was robbing herself of sharing the miracle of the life growing inside her; or the tenderness Benjamin had shown her.

'Hey,' he said softly, his thumb brushing over her cheek. 'It couldn't have been that bad.'

'What? No.' She shook her head. 'It's not—it wasn't bad.' She gave him that smile again. 'We should probably get to dinner.'

'Alexa—'

'I'm fine, Benjamin. I promise.' But she wasn't. She was promising a lie. 'We're fine, too.' That one she meant.

Because in her head, this would be the last kiss. Tonight would be the last night they spent together. Soon people would know their relationship was fake, a joke. Lee would know—but she would survive it. She would go on to court Cherise de Bruyn and focus on getting the chef, as she should have from the beginning. No one would distract her. Not even Benjamin.

At least that way, though her heart seemed to be unsure of her decisions, her head wouldn't be.

CHAPTER SEVEN

'REALLY, MOM?' SAID Benjamin when they walked in. 'You haven't even said hello but already you have baby videos out?' His mother gave him a bright smile in return, and he couldn't even be mad. He rolled his eyes though. Looked at Alexa. 'Go ahead. Clearly my mother would like to start the evening with embarrassment.'

Alexa walked past him, wearing a smile more genuine than the last few she'd given him. He didn't know if he was relieved or annoyed. Neither. Both.

'I'm going to be very disappointed if there are no videos of him running around naked,' Alexa said. 'It's the only level of embarrassment I'll accept.'

'Well, then, you're in luck,' Nina Foster said with a smile.

'It's lovely to meet you, Mrs Foster.' Alexa held out a hand.

'I've already told you my name is Nina.' His mother ignored Alexa's hand, instead pulling her in for a hug. Alexa accepted with a small laugh. Benjamin released a breath he didn't realise he'd been holding. When his mother pulled back, she said, 'You can call me Aunty Nina, dear.'

At that, Alexa grinned. 'Perfect.'

'I take it Dad's in the kitchen,' Benjamin said to distract himself from the troubling warmth in his chest.

'Yes. He's almost done though. That man loves to cook.' Nina aimed that at Alexa. 'It's where Benny gets his talent.'

'In that case, I'm looking forward to dinner.' Alexa turned to Benjamin. 'Should I hang this up, or can I drape it over a chair?'

'Oh, I've got it.'

He took the coat, went to his bedroom and hung it on a hanger from his own cupboard. It was the least he could do, considering the coat had been collateral damage in their make-out session, when he'd tossed it on the floor. He wouldn't have bothered doing anything with her coat otherwise.

His mother would have scolded him, but only after he'd already set the guest's coat down somewhere innocuous. It was the approach he took with most of his clothing, as evidenced by the tornado that had gone off in his room. His parents refused to go in there. Since he helped with the household expenses, they had a *you're an adult, you deserve your privacy* policy. Except he didn't think they meant privacy in the form of someone—including, on particularly bad days, him—being unable to find anything inside the room.

He took another look at things, winced. It would be better if Alexa—

'Is this your room?'

He turned quickly, blocking the doorway with his body. She was a little further down the passage, so she hadn't seen anything. Yet. He would keep it that way.

'Er...no. I mean, yes.' He closed the door behind him. 'It's where I...do things.'

'Things?'

'Sleep.'

'Hmm.'

'Dress.'

'Okay.' She narrowed her eyes. 'Why don't you want me to see it?'

It was obviously too much to hope that she would be polite and ignore his reluctance. But no, not Alexa. She was too straightforward, too unapologetic to allow something like politeness to get in the way of information she wanted.

'It's untidy.'

She waved a hand. 'So was mine the other day.'

'*That* was untidy?' He rolled his eyes. 'Honestly, I have no idea what that word means with some people. My mother says exactly the same thing and the place is spotless.' He paused. 'I'm willing to bet she told you our place is untidy right now. And I know for a fact she spent the entire day supervising our cleaner.'

'I wouldn't take that bet.' She lifted her nose in the air before she grinned. 'Because she just did.'

He chuckled, but stopped when she took a step forward. 'I'm not like you or my mother.'

'What does that mean?'

'When I say something's untidy, I mean it.'

'Well, so do I. I have certain standards, same as in the restaurant. If I say it's untidy, it doesn't suit those standards.' Her gaze sharpened. 'I've never been to yours. Are you saying you keep a sloppy house?'

'Of course not,' he said, offended. 'I have high standards, too.' But he winced. 'That doesn't necessarily translate to my room.'

'So what you're saying is you live in a pigsty.'

'I would not say that.'

'Let me see it, then.' She folded her arms, baiting him.

Damn her.

'I'd rather not. Did my mother send you here?' he asked without waiting to hear her reply. 'I was barely gone for a minute.'

'No. I asked to use the bathroom. What with this situation happening...' She gestured to her stomach.

'You *told* her?'

'That I needed to go to the bathroom because

I'm pregnant?' She pulled a face. 'Of course not. Why would I?'

'Oh.' He winced. 'I'm sorry. That was an over-reaction.'

She rolled her eyes. 'The bathroom?'

'That one.' He pointed to the room across the hallway.

'Thank you,' Alexa said, and walked into it.

Benjamin stood there for a beat, feeling foolish as his heart rate went back to normal. He shook his head. He needed to put this lie behind him. It was making him skittish. But when he went back to the living room to do just that, his mother was sitting with her hands interlocked over her stomach. Her eyes were closed, and to someone who didn't know her, it would seem as if she was napping. To someone who did know her...

'Mom,' he said, lowering himself in front of her. 'Why didn't you tell me you weren't feeling well?'

She opened her eyes, the tight lines of pain in the creases around them confirming his suspicion. 'I'm fine. Stop fussing.'

'Do we have to do this every time? It's been decades.'

'Exactly. Decades and I still have to tell you I'm fine.'

'But you're not fine. You're in pain.'

'Just a little, from the excitement of the day.'

'Mom...' He trailed off, sighed. 'I wish you'd told me. We could have cancelled. You could have got some rest and not put so much pressure on yourself.'

'And miss the chance to meet Alexa?'

'Mom, Alexa's not—' He broke off. Mostly because he couldn't tell her the truth when she was like this. 'Alexa's not going anywhere,' he finished lamely. 'I'd have brought her the moment you felt better.'

'Would you have?' his mother asked, her eyes tired but sharp. 'I didn't even know about her until yesterday. You never tell us about your dating life. I assumed she's your first proper girlfriend, but I don't even know if that's true.'

'It's because—'

'I had to force you to bring her here,' she interrupted him. Her eyes were flashing now, pain mingled in with the anger. 'And she's pregnant, Benny. *Pregnant.* You hid that from us.'

'What? Oh, no, Mom. She's not—'

'Your bedroom isn't that far away, Benjamin.'

She'd heard them. Damn it. Why hadn't he thought about that?

'We can talk about it when you feel better. Let me help you to bed now.'

'No.' Nina straightened, though he could see she was doing her best not to wince. 'I want to have dinner with you and get to know that woman who's going to be in our lives from now on.'

'She's not…'

He broke off, his mind spinning with how to

tell her the truth. Through it, he heard the memory of Alexa's voice asking him why he hadn't told his mother when she'd first overheard him. He should have. But he was caught by that excitement on her face, and he couldn't bear to disappoint her.

He was as much to blame for the situation they were in as Alexa was, he realised. At least this situation. And now, his mother was in pain because of him. Because of his lies.

He exhaled. 'Mom, Alexa's baby… It's not mine.'

She was intruding. She'd known it the moment she'd seen Benjamin crouching in front of his mother. When she'd heard them talk, the conversation so personal she'd had to rest a hand on her chest because her heart felt as if it was breaking, she told herself to walk away. Except she couldn't. She was too riveted by this tender side of a man she'd once called a demon.

She'd felt that tenderness during their kiss. It was what had turned the moment from a purely physical one into something emotional. So she shouldn't have been surprised that he had the capacity to be tender. But seeing it up close and personal, especially after *feeling* it up close and personal? It felt as if someone had walked into her body, gathered her emotions together and tossed them in the air like confetti at a wedding.

She was scrambling to get them back together again when his mother had told him she knew about the baby. Then he confessed it wasn't his, and said nothing about their fake relationship. She'd given him a moment to continue, to tell his mother *why* the baby wasn't his. He hadn't. He merely watched his mother gasp, lift a hand to her mouth, his face crumbling.

So Alexa threw the emotions she had just collected to the ground, and stomped over them to help Benjamin.

'Ben,' she said softly. He looked at her, his eyes ravaged with sadness. 'Let me.'

'We need to—'

'No, *I* need to.' She sent him one look to tell him to shut up, then looked at his mother. 'Benjamin isn't the father of my baby. He's just a decent man who…is decent.' She offered him a smile before sitting on the sofa opposite Nina.

'Mrs Foster… Aunty Nina… I found out I was pregnant pretty quickly. After about two weeks. Benjamin and I hadn't started dating yet, and, well… I got myself into a situation.'

She was keeping as far to the truth as possible. The fertility treatments meant she had found out she was pregnant early. When she had, she'd refused to come in to monitor the pregnancy as her specialist had advised. She wanted to have a normal pregnancy as far as possible. Since it had started out in an unusual way, monitoring things had overwhelmed her.

She also hadn't been fake dating Benjamin then.

'I didn't want to tell him when he asked me out because he seemed like a good guy. For once, I wanted a good guy in my life. I didn't tell him for the longest time. It was wrong, and selfish, and it hurt both you and him. For that, I will never forgive myself.'

She swallowed when her eyes began to prickle. Pressed a hand to her stomach because she felt alone in this deeply personal and strangely true tale she was telling Benjamin's mother. It comforted her, which sent another wave of prickling over her eyes, and she took her time before she continued.

'He hasn't known I'm pregnant very long. I think he was still deciding what to do when you found out about me. It put him in an impossible situation. He didn't want you to be disappointed, but bringing me here tonight makes it seem like he wants me and the baby, and he isn't there yet. He didn't tell you about me because he didn't want that, for either of us,' she said with a lift of her hand.

There was a long silence. Alexa didn't know if someone was waiting for her to speak, or if she was waiting for someone to speak. Eventually, Nina broke the silence.

'Knowing all this, you're still here?'

'It's an impossible situation,' she said with a small smile. 'But it's our normal. So…*normally*… I thought meeting his mother was important.'

There was another long silence. This time, Benjamin broke it.

'I'm sorry, Mom. It was never my intention to… to disappoint you.'

His mother heaved out a sigh. 'You haven't disappointed me. In fact, your behaviour with Alexa… I'd like to think *I* raised you to be someone who doesn't judge people by actions you don't agree with.'

'If it were really you,' Benjamin said slyly, 'you wouldn't judge me for my recent actions.'

Alexa bit her lip, but stopped trying to hide her smile when Nina laughed.

'You're too charming for your own good, boy.'

'I've always thought so, too,' Alexa agreed.

'Thank you,' Benjamin replied with a grin.

Nina gave them an amused look. Then she sobered. 'My son clearly cares about you, Alexa. That's enough for me.'

Alexa nodded, pressure she didn't realise was there releasing inside her. 'Thank you.'

Nina shook her head. 'I'm actually rooting for this to work out. Because at this pace, that baby of yours might be my only chance at a grandchild.'

They didn't have time to reply, as a tall man with a shock of grey hair walked into the room.

'Benjie, boy.' In the man's grin, Alexa saw Benjamin.

'Hi, Dad.'

Benjamin's father looked at their faces, frowned. 'What did I miss?'

CHAPTER EIGHT

'THIS ISN'T MY PLACE,' Alexa said, as if only now noticing he hadn't taken her back to her flat. Which was surprising, as they hadn't spoken since they'd left his house, so she hadn't been distracted. In fact, she'd been staring out of the window the entire time.

'No, it's not.'

He didn't say anything else as he drove along the gravel road that led into the quarry. Handy, because if he had, he wouldn't have heard her small gasp when he parked. He couldn't deny that part of why he'd brought her was the wow factor. The quarry was spectacular at night; on a summer's night, even more so. There was no cool breeze to chill them, no dew glazing the grass that stretched out in front of the car park. The sky was clear, the full moon illuminating things enough that he didn't have to get out his phone's torch to guide them to the water.

And really, it was the water that was the star of the quarry. It was nestled in the hollow of the rocks, stretching out in inky darkness. The moon was reflected in it, the stars, too, and it made him wonder if perhaps this was all a little too romantic. But he wanted quiet, and the quarry was quiet. He went to the back of his car, and got out the camping chairs he kept there.

'You prepared for this?' she asked when she got out of the car. 'Were you intending on bringing me here?'

'No.' He carried the chairs to his usual spot beneath the tree at the edge of the water. When he heard her behind him he said, 'I keep these in my car.'

'For this reason?'

'Exactly.'

'You bring ladies out here a lot, then?' She gave him a sly look as she lowered herself into the chair. Then she frowned. 'You'd better be prepared to help me out of this chair. It's low, and being pregnant means I have zero control over my balance.'

'So what you're saying is that I could leave you here and you'd have to stay in the chair for ever?'

'Yes,' she replied, voice dry as a badly made cake. 'That's exactly what I'm saying.'

'Good to know.' He paused. 'Better watch your attitude.'

'You know what? I don't even need your help. The grass looks pretty soft. I can tilt to the side, break my fall with my hand, and figure it out from there.'

'The grass is lower than the chair.'

'I said I'd figure it out.'

He couldn't help his laugh, though he tried to be respectful and kept it quick and low—until she joined in, which he hadn't expected. It was strange to be laughing with her, but he suspected they were relieving the tension of the night. There'd been an undercurrent during the entire meal. He didn't blame his mother for being reserved—both Alexa's news and her pain had probably occupied her mind and her body—but it meant that he'd overcompensated. The result was a strained meal where everyone pretended nothing was wrong and it was…draining.

When they stopped laughing, they lapsed into an easy silence; another surprise. But honestly, he was grateful for it. It gave him a moment to gather his thoughts, prepare his words.

'Thank you.'

'For what?'

'What you had to do with my mom. You made a difficult situation easier.'

She sighed. 'I lied.'

'Did you?'

She frowned. 'You mean, besides the fact that I kept our fake relationship going?'

'Yes, actually.'

It took some time for her to understand.

'Oh, you want to know if the stuff I said about the father of the baby's true.'

He did. But now that she said it, he felt as if he was asking too much. Maybe if he was honest with her, too…

'Look, I know I said the lies had to end. But…' He trailed off, sighed. 'At some point tonight I realised it worked for me to be in a fake relationship, too. It made my mother happy. Maybe I knew it would and that's why I let her think we were together in the first place.' It was something he'd have to think about. 'Your pregnancy complicated things, and I got scared. But your explanation made sense. Hell, it somehow made both of us look good.'

She looked at the water. 'I wouldn't say that.'

'I would.' He let it sit for a moment. 'I realised tonight the only people whose opinions I care about are my parents. So, we can keep this going for as long as we both want to.'

'You're not afraid of disappointing your mother when it ends?'

He heaved out a breath. 'I can't see an outcome that won't hurt her. I'd rather she think I tried and it didn't work out than know I lied to her.'

'Sneaky,' she commented.

'You're one to talk.'

She laughed. 'Touché.' There was a beat. 'Thank you.'

'This isn't only for you.'

For once, he believed it. He wasn't doing this only to help her. It helped him and his family, too.

It might have been strained at dinner this evening, but there'd also been light. That light had been because of Alexa. Because of what she represented to his parents.

A future that didn't only involve taking care of them.

He'd sacrifice his reputation for his parents' peace of mind.

'I know,' she said softly. 'Still. Thank you.' Silence danced between them for a few minutes. 'To answer your earlier question, I don't know what kind of guy got me pregnant.'

His brain took a moment to shift gears. 'You don't know...if he's a good guy?'

'I don't know who he is.'

'Oh.'

Sure. That was fine. She was allowed her sexual freedom. If she didn't know who she'd slept with, that was her business. Except...

No, no exceptions. He wouldn't be a judgemental jerk.

'I was waiting,' she said into the silence, 'for some kind of bigoted statement about my sex life.'

'I wouldn't dare.'

She laughed lightly. 'You were basically biting your tongue.'

'It isn't my business.'

'No, it's not.' Her laughter faded. 'Which makes why I'm telling you I was artificially inseminated by donor sperm puzzling.'

'You were artificially inseminated?' he repeated dumbly.

'Yep.' She unclasped the hands that had been locked around her knee. 'I wanted to have a baby and the available men were… Well, I suppose there were none. Whom I trusted anyway.'

'You have no male friends?'

'I don't have any…' She broke off. 'I don't have that many friends. Besides, could you imagine me asking a friend to be the father of my child?' She shuddered. 'That would be asking for trouble. Involvement. People don't tend to keep their word, so the promise that they would never encroach on the way I raised a child would be gone pretty quickly, I bet. Especially if the baby looked like the friend.'

He thought about it. 'Alternatively, you could have gone through this *with* someone. You wouldn't have to make decisions alone. You'd have support.'

'Spoken like a man who's had support his entire life.'

'Is that a criticism?'

'Not a criticism. An observation.'

'In return, then, I observe that you don't trust people.'

'An accurate observation. Trusting people isn't worth a damn.'

He tried to formulate an answer, but found himself at a loss for words. Not emotion though. He felt sorry that she'd lived a life that encouraged her to think this way. There was some rage, too, because it seemed completely unfair that he'd had parents who'd loved him and taught him the value of leaning on family and she hadn't. Or maybe it wasn't so much rage as it was guilt, because he had something she didn't.

'Don't feel sorry for me.'

'I'm not.'

'Your mother wouldn't like you lying to me.'

His face twisted. 'Are you really using my mother to make me feel guilty about this?'

'Yes. I am a smart woman who uses the tools at her disposal.'

He chuckled softly. 'Can't argue with that.'

'Finally, you learn.'

She settled back in the chair, resting her hands on her belly. It had the same protective tint as the way she'd rubbed her stomach that night in her flat. Now he knew she'd done it because she was pregnant. What he didn't know was why *he'd* done it. Why, when they'd kissed, he'd grazed her stomach and felt a rush of protectiveness he didn't know existed inside him. Need had joined so quickly and intensely that he'd had to pull back from their kiss to deal with it. To try and deny it, as he'd done the first time he'd felt that need.

'I don't feel sorry,' he said slowly, 'I feel sad.'

She didn't answer, tilting her head from side to side.

'What?' he asked.

'I'm trying to figure out whether sad is worse.'
'And?'
She looked over, eyes shining with emotion he couldn't read but knew meant something. 'It isn't.'

Without thinking about it, he reached out a hand. She stared at it, at him, looked down, then slowly took his hand. He wanted to stand up and shout for joy. He wanted to thank her for letting him in. He wanted to pull her into his arms and kiss her. Sate the heat the contact sent through his body. Instead, he squeezed and let the quiet of the evening settle over them.

It surprised him by settling the twisting of his stomach, too. He was used to the twisting, since it came whenever his mother was in pain.

When he was young, he had thought he could do something about it. His mother would be in bed, curled up to favour whichever side of her was aching more, and he'd bring her tea. Make her food. Offer to run a bath for her, or cuddle her until she felt better. She'd never accept, and she'd apologise afterwards. She'd tell him the version of her who was in pain wasn't really *her*.

Throughout her illness, she'd tried to separate the person who was in pain and the one who wasn't. Which he understood. Her illness had been relatively unknown in South Africa when she'd been diagnosed, and even the dialogue with her doctors had separated those identities. But he knew, even as a kid, that the same mother who couldn't move some days was the mother who would spend hours reading to him. Or taking him to some exciting place he wanted to see. Or answering all his questions with patience and honesty. As he grew older, he realised his mother had separated who she was because she saw her body as her enemy during her flare-ups. It was separate for her; it was separate *from* her. It was betraying her.

He'd wanted to help her because he wanted her to remember he loved all of her, even if she couldn't do it herself. It was a big burden for a kid to undertake, even though he hadn't completely understood it. And it had evolved as he got older. Now, he tried to nudge instead of directly say. He tried to support instead of fix. It was navigating a minefield—a stubborn minefield—but since there weren't any explosions, at least not yet, Benjamin thought he was doing pretty okay. As long as he was there, he would keep doing okay.

'Is your mom going to be all right?'

He frowned, trying to remember if he'd spoken out loud and the question had been provoked. He was sure he hadn't, which meant Alexa was simply curious. He sighed in relief.

'Yeah, she'll be fine.'

'Is she unwell?'

He took a breath. 'She has something called fibromyalgia. It's a—'

'I know what it is.' At his surprised look, she

rolled her eyes. 'People are more open about chronic illnesses these days.'

'But… I mean, it's not something you just know.'

'I didn't,' she agreed. 'Until I went to look it up after seeing an acquaintance talk about it online.'

He kept his mouth shut because if he didn't he was sure he'd make inelegant grunts she'd make fun of.

'It sounds tough,' she said softly. 'Living your life in pain the whole time. I can't imagine.' There was a short pause. 'I *can* imagine how hard it must have been for you.'

He gave her a sharp look, dropping her hand in the process. She didn't seem fazed, only folding her hands over her stomach again.

'What do you mean?' he asked.

'Well, you're the kind of person who agrees to be in a fake relationship with his mortal enemy because you were feeling protective. At least, I guess that was how you were feeling? Maybe it was indignant at how Lee dared to act towards me. I can't tell with you.' She shrugged. 'Regardless, you're someone who does things when other people seem vulnerable. I'm guessing you see your mother's pain as her being vulnerable, which makes you want to do something. Except you can't, because it's *her* pain.'

It was remarkably astute. Uncomfortably astute. Which was why he said, 'No.'

The corners of her lips twitched. 'Hmm…'

'It's been fine for me.'

'Okay.'

'She's the one in pain.'

'Sure.'

'Is it hard for me to see her that way? Sure. But is it worse for me? No.'

'That's not what I said though. I know it's worse for her. Of course it is.' She paused. 'I might be off base here, what with having a messed-up family situation myself, but I don't think it would be easy for me to see someone I care about in pain.'

'It's…not.'

'I don't doubt it.' There was a long pause as the words washed over them. 'It's not an excuse for you not to pick up after yourself though. How do you even find anything in your room? It looks like the aftermath of a police search.'

As soon as the surprise faded—though he should have known she'd look—he started laughing. 'It's organised chaos.'

'Rubbish!'

'It's not rubbish.'

'You're telling me you know where every T-shirt is placed? Every shirt? Pants?'

'Exactly.'

'So if I hid something in there you'd find it?'

'Did you hide something in my room?'

She gave him a sly look. 'Maybe.'

'Alexa,' he nearly growled.

'What?' She blinked at him innocently. 'You said it's organised chaos. I'd just like to prove, once and for all, on behalf of everyone who's been sceptical about organised chaos, that that's non-sense.'

'You're trying to trap me on behalf of an entire group of people?'

'Sometimes your actions have to be bigger than yourself.'

He shook his head, but even his disbelief couldn't overshadow his amusement. Then he thought of something.

'How did you know I'd say organised chaos though?'

'Please. I've spent years trying to avoid inter-acting with you. It hasn't worked—' she sent him an accusatory look '—but at least I got to know who you are.'

He sighed. 'What did you hide in my room?'

'A handkerchief.'

'You carry a handkerchief?'

'Yes.' She sniffed. 'It's for the essential oils I carry in my purse, too. In case I have an overbear-ing bout of nausea.'

'Efficient.'

'Thanks.'

'Can you at least tell me what the handkerchief looks like?'

'Pink. Like my dress.'

'That should make it easier to find.'

'It'll be a breeze. You know where everything is, remember?'

She patted his hand, winked at his glare, and he turned away before he could smile again.

He couldn't say whether it was the teasing that soothed him, but the anxiety in his body had stopped humming. Except it couldn't be the teasing. She'd done plenty of that before, though it had lost its snarkiness at some point over the last few days.

As he thought about it, he realised it was that she understood. His position in his family had always made him feel alone, and finally he didn't feel that way any more.

He let it wash over him. Didn't even question that Alexa had been the one to make him feel that way—or what it meant. Still, he couldn't let her get the upper hand.

'So,' he said casually, 'are we going to talk about that kiss?'

'What kiss?'

He snorted. 'There's no way you don't—'

'What kiss, Benjamin?'

At her tone, he looked over. Saw her determination. It made him laugh, which turned the determination into a glare. Satisfied that he'd won, he stood and offered a hand to help her up.

CHAPTER NINE

ALEXA WALKED INTO the restaurant and saw him immediately.

'You've got to be kidding me,' she muttered, pausing.

It had been a few days since she and Benjamin had had *that* moment. It wasn't a defined moment. She couldn't say—oh, this thing happened and things have changed. Besides the kisses. And the fact that she thought he might be nice, despite the whole stealing-her-chef thing. Or how kind he was with his parents; how eager he was to please them. All she knew for sure was that at some point at the quarry, things had shifted. She needed time to sort through it, and she had other things to do first.

Such as secure her chef before she went on maternity leave.

There was time. She was days away from entering her second trimester, so she had about six months. That was what she told herself logically. In reality, she was freaking out. Hiring a new chef was a nightmare. She knew because she'd done so months before and it had all gone to hell anyway. So she needed time to find the right person, make sure they worked well with the rest of her team. Train them to work for Infinity, with her and with Kenya. She had to be there to observe and make sure everything would go smoothly when she was away.

She only had six months to do so.

No wonder she had indigestion.

That could have been her pregnancy, too, but she had a feeling being stressed about the new chef didn't help. Or being at odds with Kenya, who'd stubbornly refused to talk about anything other than work in the last week. Usually, Kenya was a champagne bottle, shaken and uncorked and overflowing with personal anecdotes. Now she was a bottle of wine; one that was aging and still and not overflowing with anything.

It was hard for Alexa to believe she missed all of Kenya's energy and her much too personal stories about her life. But she did. And now she had to deal with realising she missed the connection of it, too, and think about how to fix it, and about why Kenya was really so mad at her. She did *not* need to face Benjamin and his kissable lips today.

She marched over to the table.

'You're stealing my appointments with Cherise now, too?'

He looked up, smiled at her, and did it all so

slowly that it felt as though someone had pushed a button for that to happen. Her heart did a little skip at that face; her mind recognised that his surprise, his pleasure at seeing her were genuine.

'Hey!' He stood. 'You have an appointment with Cherise, too?'

'Too?' She looked at the table. There were only two seats. 'How can we both have an appointment with her?'

He shrugged. 'She called me the day before yesterday to ask me if I could meet her here.' He gestured at the restaurant. It was perfectly nice with black and white décor, some greenery courtesy of plants, and the faint smell of fish because of its position near the water of the V&A Waterfront. 'Said it would be a nice neutral space.'

Alexa huffed out a breath. 'Yeah, because that's what I told her. After I called her the day before yesterday to ask for this meeting.'

He blinked. 'You called Cherise after we spent the night together?'

'I'm not sure I'd describe dinner with your family as us spending the night together, but yes, I did.' She straightened her spine. 'You said we should continue with our plans as usual.'

'Yeah, but I didn't expect—'

He frowned. Shoved his hands into his pockets. Suddenly she noticed that he was wearing a shirt. She'd seen him in one before, but now he looked... different. His shoulders were broad, chest defined, the material clinging to all of it. She half expected him to move and tear through a perfectly good piece of clothing.

Why was a part of her cheering for that to happen?

'I guess she wanted to speak with both of us at the same time.'

'I did,' Cherise said from beside them. Alexa nearly jumped out of her skin.

'How long have you been there?'

'Just arrived,' Cherise replied. 'Sorry to spring this on you.' She narrowed her eyes. 'Although I was sure I wouldn't actually be able to do that, since you two are dating.'

There was a beat as Alexa realised she was going to have to pretend again. Fortunately, Benjamin spoke before she could say anything.

'We keep our personal and professional lives separate.' He smiled, oozing charm. Alexa nearly slipped on the puddle of it before she realised this was what he did. He charmed people. But *not* her. Especially not if she continued ignoring the fact that they'd kissed. 'Thought it for the best, considering we're in the same business.'

'I imagine that must help. Or make things more complicated, if you're meeting up like this.'

'It doesn't happen as often as you'd think,' Alexa answered Cherise. Cherise gave her a rueful smile.

'I thought it might be easier to discuss this together.' She paused. 'In hindsight, I suppose I was using your relationship to make things easier for myself. I wouldn't have to have two meetings about possibly the same thing. I'm blurring things for you,' she added with a frown.

'Don't worry about it,' Benjamin said smoothly. 'We're mature enough to handle it.'

He sent Alexa a look as if to say *I'm mature enough*. It took all of Alexa's willpower not to roll her eyes at him, or stick out her tongue. Or do anything really that would undermine her maturity. She could be mature.

'Should we get someone to add a chair to this table?' Alexa asked coolly. Maturely. She gestured to a waiter. 'I booked a two-seater.'

'This is the table I booked, actually,' Benjamin said, also gesturing to the waiter. When he looked at Alexa, she pulled a face. *This is you being mature?*

'Oh, I booked a table for three,' Cherise interjected. 'I just saw you two here and came directly to speak to you. I'll have the waiter take us.'

Soon they were sitting together and ordering drinks.

'So,' Cherise started, 'I know whatever either of you wanted to say to me today probably isn't going to work out because the other crashed the lunch.'

She and Benjamin exchanged a look. They hadn't *crashed* the lunch. Cherise had invited

Benjamin to an appointment Alexa and she had agreed on. If anything, Cherise had done the crashing. By proxy.

Acid pushed up in Alexa's chest. She'd done a lot of research to find Cherise. Her first step had been to call her old mentor at the restaurant she'd worked at after the Institute. He'd recommended two people, one of whom was studying at the same institute she'd studied at—Cherise—the other of whom was still working for him, but was looking for something more, more urgently than what he could offer.

It had taken her a while to find out that Cherise wasn't studying at the Institute as a newbie who wanted to learn everything she could. No, Cherise had worked under the best chefs, her old mentor included, for almost a decade, and had decided to formalise her knowledge by getting an official qualification. She was interested in something new, which, after speaking with some of the people Cherise had worked with, including the instructors they had in common, Alexa was eager to offer.

Except now it seemed Cherise wasn't going to be that good a match after all.

'I thought I'd say some things to both of you instead,' Cherise said. 'One: I would be happy to work with either of you. I'm looking for something different to what I've done in the past, which tended to lean towards more traditional fine dining. Nothing wrong with it,' she added quickly, 'but I'd like to do something more creative than cauliflower purée. I'm eager to explore that creativity, and I believe your restaurants, both younger, trendier places, would give me the space to do that.'

Alexa rubbed the burning in her chest thoughtfully. It wasn't subsiding, though her doubts about Cherise were. Perhaps that was enough for now.

'Two: I have no idea which one of you I'd like to work for.' Cherise gave them a small smile. 'I've dined at both your restaurants. Both of them were amazing experiences, and each of your spaces I respond to. Yours is more traditional, with the wood and the partitions between each side of the restaurant,' she said to Benjamin, 'but there's something about it that makes me nostalgic. Yet I love how modern Infinity is,' Cherise continued, speaking to Alexa now. 'It's sleek, and so not where I'd expect to be served fine dining.'

'Thank you…?'

Cherise laughed. 'It's a compliment,' she assured Alexa. 'You've brought a younger crowd in by modernising your place, and I respect someone who can instil respect for good food in a generation that fast food was basically designed for.'

'Well, then, thank you,' Alexa said more firmly. 'The conclusion I've come to is that it will depend on who I get along with the best. The only way I can know that is to spend more time with you both.'

'Of course,' Alexa said. 'You can come to the restaurant any time you'd like. I can show you around, have you speak with some of my staff. I'm sure Benjamin would allow that, too.'

'Sure.'

'And I'd love that. But I was thinking of something a little different.'

'What?'

She wrinkled her nose. 'School.'

'Why do I feel like we were being interviewed?' Benjamin asked minutes after Cherise had left the restaurant.

'Not were,' Alexa corrected. 'Are. We now have to take a three-day course at the Institute. Which I don't mind per se, it's just…' Her voice faded and she let out a huge sigh.

'Everything okay?'

'Fine.'

But she dropped her head onto a hand she'd rested on the table.

If his instincts hadn't already been tingling from that sigh, this would have done them in. In fact, it felt as though an alarm was going off in his head. It dimmed the sound of the inner voice warning him not to get involved. Things were already almost impracticably complicated between them; he didn't need to further complicate that by getting involved with her issues.

Except she looked so fragile, sitting there with her hand on her head. It was so different to how she usually seemed—abrasive, bull-headed, *strong*—that he had to fight harder than he would have liked not to ask. And then he found himself fighting against *that* because he did want to ask. Hell, he even wanted to make it better. Which was exactly how things usually went wrong. People would take advantage of his tendency to take over. After he'd had a 'friend' do it recently, he'd learnt his lesson.

He eyed Alexa.

'You okay?' he asked anyway, because he was a fool who hadn't learnt a thing.

'I've already said I'm fine,' she said, but there was no heat in the words. If she were feeling herself, there definitely would have been heat in the words.

'It's just that—' he tried not to show his surprise that she'd continued '—this is turning out to be a lot harder than I thought it would be. Everything is,' she said in an uncharacteristically small voice as she lifted her head. 'I wanted to get Cherise to work for me so I could go on maternity leave without worrying I was ruining my restaurant by having a baby. Leaving it vulnerable in some way. Maybe even to you and Lee. Now I have to do this course with you.' She looked up at him. Her eyes were gleaming, but sharp. 'No offence.'

He wondered if he should dignify that with a response.

'Why can't anything be simple?' she whispered now. 'Why can't I have a family that doesn't suck? Why couldn't my chef have stayed on so that I wouldn't have this stress during my pregnancy? Why couldn't...?'

She exhaled. Waved a hand.

'I'm fine.'

'Clearly.'

She gave him a dark look. He preferred it to the sadness.

'I can't help you with—'

'Any of it,' she interrupted. 'You can't help me with any of it. But I appreciate the effort.'

'I wasn't going to say that.'

'Oh, I know,' she said, straightening now. She took a deep sip of water, but kept her gaze on him. 'I know what you were going to say, Benjamin. It was going to be about what you could help me with. You might even have been considering stepping out of this race with Cherise because things would be easier for me then.'

'I wasn't—'

She cut him off with a single raised eyebrow. And because, of course, he *was*.

'Where would it leave you, Benjamin?' she asked softly. 'You'd have to look for another chef.

You'd have to answer to my brother. You're clearly letting your personal feelings override how you feel professionally.'

'There are no personal feelings.'

She looked at him strangely. The confusion cleared in seconds.

'Oh, no, I don't mean *for* me. Of course not.' There was a beat. 'I meant you're letting your desire to fix things for people cloud your professional opinion. Which should be that you should do that three-day course and fight to have her work for you.'

She grabbed her purse, threw some notes onto the table.

'That's what I'll be doing.'

Then she was gone.

He sat, bemused, until the waiter came to the table, saw the money Alexa had left, and asked if he wanted the bill. He said yes, stuffed her notes in his wallet, and paid with his card. Then he walked. Not to his car, where he probably should have gone. He had work to do.

But his thoughts demanded that he pay them heed, and he couldn't do that when he was driving, or working. So he walked. Away from the bustle of the Waterfront, where tourists shopped and locals ate. Down, past the docks, until he was simply walking along the edge of the Waterfront, waves splashing against the rocks beyond the railing.

The conversation he'd had with Alexa…

Well, he couldn't exactly call it a conversation. More a monologue, with the occasional pauses. He couldn't be upset with her though; she was right. There'd been a moment, and not a brief one, where he'd thought about giving up the fight for Cherise.

A lot about that bothered him. The first was, simply, that it was stupid. He'd spent a long time trying to find her. Speaking with his contacts at restaurants she'd worked in and at the Institute. Making sure she had the skills a chef in his kitchen would need.

He'd started out as the head chef, back when Lee had reached out to him years ago. Though that was tainted now with the knowledge that Lee had done it to get back at Alexa, Benjamin could still recognise his luck. Because Lee had been the one to help him make the transition once he'd discovered his passion went beyond the kitchen.

Since Lee had multiple businesses, he couldn't invest much time in the restaurant. So when Benjamin had decided to switch gears and spoken to Lee about his desire to branch out, Lee had offered to train him. For two years, they'd done just that. This was the first year he'd taken on the responsibility fully, and he wanted to make Lee proud. Hell, he wanted to make himself proud. Giving away his chance because he wanted to help out a woman who didn't need his help was definitely stupid.

The second thing that bothered him about wanting to was that she'd seen through him. She had the uncanny ability to do so, which she'd displayed at lunch today and at the quarry the other night. He could blame the ability on the fact that she didn't seem to want his help. Despite what he'd first thought about her, Alexa wasn't using him. If she was, she would have said it by now. She was disturbingly honest like that.

Which was why he couldn't be dishonest with himself when it came to her. She didn't see through him because she didn't want his help. Well, not only because of that. It was also because she knew him, could see him, and he didn't like it.

He had a persona to maintain. An important one. The moment his parents realised he felt responsible for looking after them, they'd stop him from doing so. The moment his mother saw that he'd seen another future for himself because of the fake relationship with Alexa, she'd do anything she could for him to have it.

But he couldn't have it. It wasn't compatible with living at home, helping his father around the house, spending time with his mother. If Alexa saw through him, she might see the things he didn't want anyone knowing, too. What if she mentioned it to his mother? To his father? And just because she wasn't using him now didn't mean she never would. Look at what his friends had done. His cousins.

They pretended to spend time with him, be his friend, but they only wanted things. Money, free food, help with an event. It was predictable in its consistency. As predictable as his ability to fall for it. Because they needed him.

He had reasons to stay away from Alexa. To not give in to the pull he felt between them. Good reasons. Professional *and* personal reasons. He only had one reason to see her: he had to get Cherise to work for him.

One more reason, a voice in his head reminded him. He almost groaned.

Yes, he had one more reason to see her. He was also supposed to be in a relationship with her.

CHAPTER TEN

A FORTNIGHT LATER Alexa arrived at the Institute early, ready to get the first day of the course over with. Perhaps not a winning attitude, but the best one she could muster under the circumstances. She'd been to the doctor the day before for her thirteen-week appointment. Apparently, she'd been blessed with twins.

It did not seem like a blessing at that moment.

She'd known it was a possibility, of course. She'd read many articles about fertility treatments; her doctor had pretty much repeated the information to her verbatim. But she hadn't once considered that *she'd* have twins. Twins weren't for someone who needed to find a chef for her business so it wouldn't fail or be vulnerable to attacks by a sibling or for someone who didn't know how to raise one child, let alone two. *Two!* What had she done to deserve this?

Well, a voice in her brain said, quite reasonably, *you're at odds with your family. You're pretending to date a man and lying to the people you care about. Your only friend isn't talking to you because of the lie, and you refuse to tell her the truth. You also haven't told her you're pregnant— with twins—and you've pushed away anyone who could possibly come to care about you.*

It was a long list of her flaws. Surprisingly long, considering her own head had provided them. Although that the list was there at all wasn't a surprise. She wasn't perfect. The fact that she was prickly, bull-headed, and stubborn wasn't news. But since those characteristics had helped her survive her family and build her business, she could see the good in them, too.

So maybe twins were her punishment for her irreverence.

Not that her children were a punishment. Of course not.

'Sorry,' she murmured to them. 'I'm just surprised. And worried. What if I'm not a good mother to you? There are two of you now, so I'll be screwing up twice as much.'

She let out a huge breath, and sipped the herbal tea she'd bought before she'd left for the Institute. The warmth of it gave her some much-needed comfort. The rap on her window did not—nor did seeing who it was.

She opened the window. 'I'll be sending you my hospital bills.'

Benjamin gave her a half-smile, almost as if he

expected her to give him a hard time. Almost as if he liked it. 'For what?'

'My heart attack.'

She grabbed her things, closed the window, and got out of the car. He hadn't moved far away, so when she turned, she found herself in his bubble. His musky scent didn't make her nauseous, as she'd expected it to, since it was in the window of her morning illness time. Maybe because her other body parts had woken up and decided to respond to it.

When she'd read that pregnancy would make her more…sensitive, she'd laughed. She hadn't been sensitive to anyone in such a long time. She couldn't even remember who the last person she'd been sensitive to was. And yet what she was feeling now was anything but amusement. She was incredibly aware of the smell of him. Incredibly aware of his body only centimetres from hers.

He looked delicious in his black T-shirt and jeans; his standard outfit in the kitchen, even when they'd been studying. Again, she noticed his shoulders, his chest. His body was muscular and strong and she wondered what it would be like if he scooped her into his arms. Would she feel light, even now, pregnant with twins? Would she be annoyed that he'd dare do it?

Or would she be amused, attracted? A playful combination of both that would have her inching forward to kiss him…?

'Oh,' she said, and leaned back against the car.

'Are you okay?' he asked, moving even closer.

'Yeah. You're just…um…awfully close.'

He looked down, seemingly only noticing it now. His lips curved into a smile that had her heart racing. Not because it was sexy and sly. Of course not. It was because she knew what that slyness meant.

'Are you having a tough time because I'm close to you, Alexa?'

Oh, no. He was speaking in a low voice that was even more seductive than the smile.

'No.' She cleared her throat when the word came out huskily. 'I'm having a hard time because I'm pregnant. I need air and space and… stuff,' she finished lamely.

It was a pity. He'd believed her until she'd said that. Now he was smirking, which was quite annoying. But it gave her an idea.

'It's probably good that I'm close to you though. I'm so dizzy.'

She braced herself, then rested her head on his chest. The bracing didn't help. Not when his arms automatically went around her, holding her tighter against him. His heart thudded against her cheek, her own heart echoing. She closed her eyes as she realised her mistake.

'It's okay,' he said softly. 'I've got you.'

The words had a lump growing in her throat. She looked up, defiantly, she thought, because she didn't need him to *have* her. But she completely melted at his expression. It was soft and concerned and protective. Then he ran the back of his finger over her cheek, his gaze slipping to her lips, and she was melting, all right, but for the wrong reasons.

'I should...sit down.'

'Yeah,' he said shakily, stepping away.

He'd been as affected as she had.

She wrapped her hands around her cup. How was she still holding it? How hadn't she dumped it all over Benjamin? She began to walk over the strip of stones that separated the car park and the grass. They settled on the bench under a large tree metres away, and she sighed at the view of the vineyard. Bright green and dark green with the brown of the sand stretching out in front of them. At the very end of the vineyard rose a mountain; tall and solid, it enclosed the area and made everything seem private. With the quiet of the early morning settling over them, Alexa realised she hadn't come early to get the day over with as much as she'd come for this.

She could remember the days she'd done the same thing when she'd been studying. She'd still been living at home, paying her parents for the pleasure with the little she earned working part-time as a kitchen hand. She couldn't wait to escape to this beautiful place every weekday. Away from the attention her parents had lavished on her about her goals in life. Goals that weren't aligned with the ones they'd had for her life, which was why they had kept pushing.

Pushing and pushing, until she had been sure she would fall over from the stress of it.

'Is it better now?'

'Hmm?' She looked over at him. Blinked. 'Oh, the dizziness? Yes. Tons.'

He smiled, but apparently knew better than to comment. 'What distracted you just now?'

'I used to love coming here early. It's so beautiful, and peaceful.' She exhaled, forcing out the bad memories that came with the good ones.

'It really is something,' he agreed. Except he was looking at her. Intensely.

She cleared her throat. 'Is…um…is this why you're here so early?'

'You know what they say. Early bird gets the best view.'

'And maybe the station third from the front.' She laughed at his expression. 'We all know that one's the best.'

'Not true. Station seven is.'

'Station seven's left stove plate can't simmer.'

He laughed. 'How do you know this place so well?'

'You mean, how is it that you can't fool me?' She gave him an amused look. 'I pay attention.'

'Yeah,' he said softly. 'You do.'

Somehow, she didn't think he was referring to

the stove. She sipped her tea instead of asking him, and nearly spat it out again when he said, 'You've grown.'

Swallowing it back down proved challenging.

'What do you mean?'

'Your stomach is bigger,' he said quickly. Which, of course, she'd known, but it was worth asking the question for that look of panic on his face. She hid her smile with another sip of tea.

'Yes. This happens when you're expecting.'

'It's only been two weeks. Is it supposed to grow so quickly?'

She laughed lightly. 'I hope so. But my doctor is happy with everything. I saw her yesterday. I guess growing fast is what happens when you're expecting two.'

Maybe a part of her had known he would react this way. Multiple blinks, mouth opening and closing, every muscle she could see frozen. He was in shock, and it felt like a vindication of her own reaction. It even made her want to laugh at her own reaction, which was probably as comical as his. No—most likely more. She was the one carrying the twins.

'Two? As in twins?'

She merely raised her brows in answer.

'Of course it's twins. Two are twins.' He stood, began to pace. 'You're sure?'

Though she hadn't quite anticipated *this* reaction, she nodded, eager to see where it would go.

'Man. Twins? *Twins.*' His long legs easily strode back and forth over the distance in front of the bench. 'I can't believe you're having two.'

'I couldn't either,' she said slowly, 'and I'll actually be the one giving birth to them. Raising them.'

It took him a few moments, but he seemed to understand the implication. He stopped, gave her a sheepish smile.

'Sorry. I guess for a moment there I was...' He broke off, confusion crossing his face. 'I don't know what I was doing.'

'Maybe you imagined what it would be like if we really were dating,' she offered. 'Think about it. You started dating a woman who was pregnant, something you didn't sign up for, but you're too good a guy to let that keep you from developing a relationship with her. So, hey, maybe you can be a father to one kid if you liked one another enough. But two?' She gave a slight shake of the head. 'That would freak anyone out.'

'Even you?'

She laughed. It sounded a little deranged even to her own ears. Not that that kept her from answering.

'I always wanted a family. A good one, I mean. I realised about a year ago that I could only create that for myself. I couldn't rely on my own family for that.' She stared at that green in the distance, letting herself speak. She needed to say it out loud. 'I thought someday I'd have another. I'd teach them to cherish one another. To be each other's best friend, not competition. Not like my relationship with Lee. They would be different, how I dreamt siblings would be—always there for each other, so they would always know love.'

She rested her hands on her stomach. On the two lives growing there.

'But I would have time between them. Two right away? It's scary. What if I'm not cut out for this?'

She exhaled sharply; shook her head sharply. Now wasn't the time to have a breakdown. She'd only found out about the twins the day before, and clearly she needed to process. But she wouldn't do it now, in front of him. Well, *more* in front of him than she already had done. She wouldn't say anything about her fear of her restaurant failing. Or failing the people who relied on her there. Less because she felt it—although she did—and more because she knew he'd feel sorry for her. Based on his expression now, he already did. And her pregnancy didn't even involve him.

She inhaled now. Offered him a smile. 'But no, I'm not freaking out.'

He smiled back, because she was vulnerability wrapped up in fire and he wanted to burn himself so badly. He couldn't help it. The combination of her traits—traits that were polar opposites in everyone but her, that made her who she was—was so appealing. Fascinating. Intriguing.

Even as he thought it, he shook his head. How could he find her appealing? Fascinating? Intriguing? He'd just thought—seconds ago—that she was vulnerable. Vulnerability meant she would need someone. It put her in the perfect position to use someone. And that someone couldn't be him.

Mainly because something inside him, *everything* inside him, wanted it to be him.

He'd been trained for this, hadn't he? He'd spent years managing his mother's vulnerabilities. Not that they needed to be managed, he thought with a frown. His mother's pain wasn't a problem he needed to solve; he knew that. It was just... He'd had to manage his reaction to it. He had to be the person she needed during her bad times, which meant he couldn't take over and demand she do what he wanted her to, no matter how strong the urge. He had to support her without overwhelming her. It was the hardest thing he'd ever done. But he'd done it. He was good at it. Maybe that was why he was so attracted to Alexa—he could be good at managing himself with her, too.

'Good thing,' he replied, unwilling, or maybe unable, to dive into the mess of his thoughts. 'If you were freaking out about it, I wouldn't be able to reassure you.'

She gave him a bland look. He chuckled.

'There's nothing wrong with accepting reassurance.'

'But I don't need to,' she said, voice full of emotion, though she was desperately trying to control it, 'because I'm not freaking out.'

'A logical reaction to your news.'

'Hmm.'

'Not freaking out. Who would freak out, finding out they were going to have two children when they were expecting one?' He sat down beside her. 'I'm going to be honest with you: you don't have to worry about being a bad mother. There's no way.'

He wanted to reach out and take her hand, but it felt too intimate. Then he did it anyway, because his gut told him to and he wasn't going to think about where that gut feeling was coming from.

'It's okay to feel jolted by this. I think anyone would. But your reaction now doesn't mean you'll be a bad mother.'

'I didn't think…' She broke off. Looked at him. 'I did.'

He smiled. 'I know. But you're strong-minded. Kind when it counts. Resilient. You'll get through having two.'

'You sound sure about that.'

'I am. You've built a restaurant from the ground up, Alexa. It's successful because of you. Surely raising two kids can't be much harder.'

He winked at her, and she smiled despite the

emotion running wild over her face. Then it disappeared.

'What did I say?'

'Nothing. You were doing a perfectly adequate job of comforting me.'

He chuckled. 'As long as it was adequate.'

'Thank you.'

She squeezed his hand. Then, without warning, she leaned forward and kissed him. It was over before he could react, the only evidence it had happened the tingling at his lips.

She stood. 'You can't see that I'm pregnant, can you? I mean, I know *you* can, but as someone who didn't know?'

He opened his mouth. Closed it. Lowered his eyes because what else could he do? He tried to focus on her question. What had she asked him? Oh, yes, her clothes.

She was wearing… He didn't quite know what. It was a brightly coloured piece of material that was draped over her front from left to right. It did wonders for her cleavage, and he had to wrench his gaze away to answer her question. The material hung loosely over her stomach, and, paired with her tights and trainers, made her look both chic and comfortable. And not pregnant.

'You can't tell. It's loose enough that if I didn't know you were pregnant, I'd think…'

He broke off, but it was too late.

'You'd think what?'

He shook his head.

'You'd better say it, Foster.'

He shook his head again, this time more vehemently.

'You're saying that if people didn't know I was pregnant they'd think I was putting on weight?'

'I did *not* say that.'

'Only because you thought better of it.'

But her chest was shaking, and soon, sound joined.

'You think this is funny?' he asked.

'*You're* funny.'

'Wow. Thanks.'

She shrugged. Patted him on the shoulder. 'I appreciate that you wanted to preserve my feelings. But honestly, I don't care what people think of my body. As long as I feel good and everything works like it's supposed to, weight isn't important to me.'

He opened his mouth, then closed it when he realised he had nothing to add to that. It was a healthy way to think of the body, and, because he knew how prevalent weight-watching was in their culture, very enlightened.

'Yeah,' he said. 'You don't have to worry about being a mother, Alexa. You'll do fine.'

Her surprised look made the compliment well worth it.

CHAPTER ELEVEN

HE'D BEEN COOKING his entire life. It started because he wanted to be exactly like his father when he was younger. It continued because he wanted to make his parents' lives easier after his mother's diagnosis. She couldn't work at his father's business for periods of time, and during those periods his father had been overwhelmed at work. At least until he realised a temp could solve his problems. In any case, Benjamin had taken the opportunity before his father had realised that to make himself useful in the kitchen at home.

He hadn't known much at that point, and dinner had often been some form of a sandwich. Then he'd moved on to pasta, which had seemed doable for a boy under ten. He began to study his father more seriously, helping with the harder tasks. By the time he was a teenager, he could fry a steak with the best of them. Soon after, he was adding sauces and presenting meals he saw on the cooking shows he'd come to love. When he had to decide what he wanted to do with his life, it seemed natural to go into professional cooking.

Except he didn't get into culinary school the first year. Or the second, or third. Competition was steep, and he had nothing to give him an edge. He spent the years he wasn't cooking getting a degree in financial management, thinking he could at least help his father out if he couldn't have his dream. When he graduated, he'd pretty much given up on the Institute. Until his parents sat him down and told him he deserved to give it one more try if it truly was what he wanted to do with his life.

He spent the two years after that in kitchens of different restaurants, wherever would have him. Sometimes he got work as a kitchen assistant; sometimes he washed the dishes. But he always, always tried to learn from those in charge. And eventually, the fourth time he applied, he got into the Institute.

And not once in all that time, and during all those experiences, had he thought baking was for him.

Today proved that.

'I didn't realise the course was going to be about decorating,' he said casually.

Cherise was beside him, putting buttercream into several separate bowls so she could colour them for her rainbow cake.

'Yeah,' she said, 'I thought it would be fun. And,

since it's the Institute's only short course, it worked.' She looked at him. 'Are you having trouble?'

'Not at all.'

He'd already coloured his buttercream, which he knew would be the easiest part of his day. He hadn't done anything more than that because it would have entailed showing his weaknesses, and he preferred not to parade those if he could help it.

Cherise smiled. 'This isn't a test to see whether you can decorate a cake. I'm aware you probably don't need those skills at the restaurant.'

He took a beat, then realised it was best to be honest. 'It's not that I don't need the skills. It's that I don't have them, no matter how hard I try.'

Her smile widened. 'Well, then, today should be fun for you.'

'Not sure that's the word I'd use.'

She laughed and her focus went back to her cake. He sighed and did the same with his. But not before he sneaked a look at Alexa, who stood on the other side of Cherise. She was already on the second layer of her cake, and looked as comfortable with the task as she did with any other. It was part of the problem he'd had with her when they were studying together. Nothing seemed to faze her. No task, no matter how ridiculous, pulled the rug out from under her.

Back then, he hadn't appreciated how easily she found everything. It had simply seemed unfair that she would have skill with everything in the kitchen. Now, at least, he could admire that skill. Except he saw that Cherise was admiring it, too.

It frustrated him, almost as much as it had in the past—except now feelings were creeping in.

He tried to tell himself he was just a sucker who couldn't resist someone who needed his help. It was clear Alexa did, even if she didn't think so. And he could easily be like her brother, using his vulnerabilities, his desires, to get what she wanted.

A voice in his head told him he had it all wrong. He didn't listen, instead focusing on getting his cake decorated as best he could. It took much more concentration and precision than he would have liked, but when he was done, he was proud of what he'd created.

'Nice job,' Cherise commented.

'Thanks.' He wiped his forehead with an arm. 'It was hard work.'

She laughed. 'Worth it though, don't you think, Alexa?'

Alexa peered past Cherise, appraising his cake before looking at him. 'It looks good.'

That's it. That's all she said. There was no judgement, no praise. Just an honest statement and yet somehow, it made him mad. He was sure she'd decorated her cake with a fraction of the effort he had put into his own. And now she had the cheek to tell him his looked good?

He wasn't being logical. A part of him recognised it. But he leaned into the irrationality of his thoughts, letting it fuel him for the rest of the day. He worked through lunch, though he knew it was silly, considering he was there to get to know Cherise. As far as he could tell, though, it seemed as if Cherise was more interested in chatting with him during their working sessions. Alexa was oddly quiet, though when he glanced out of the window during lunch, he saw her and Cherise laughing about something.

He gritted his teeth, did what he had to do, and at the earliest moment he could he walked out of the doors. Seconds later, footsteps followed him.

'Hey,' Alexa said. 'Wait up.'

He kept walking.

'Benjamin,' she said, her voice exasperated. 'I'm pregnant. There are two people growing inside me. Please don't make me run after you.'

That forced him to slow down, but he didn't stop. He was afraid of what would happen if he stopped. He was well aware he was in a mood. He also knew his mood was tied up in her, in both good and bad ways, except he couldn't discern between the two at the moment. It didn't bode well for their conversation. So when she caught up with him, he decided to stay quiet.

'Cherise wanted to know what's wrong with you.' Alexa rubbed her stomach. 'She asked me like she expected me to know. But I didn't know, and I had to pretend to, because we're together and when you're in a mood, apparently, I need to be able to explain that.'

'What did you say?' he couldn't help but ask.

'That you're competitive. And a perfectionist. When you put the two together, it can be a damning combination.'

'So you bad-mouthed me.'

'Not entirely,' she said easily, ignoring his bad temper. 'I also said it makes you a hell of an entrepreneur. You want to give your patrons the best. It makes you serious, disagreeable perhaps, but it also makes you one of the best people she could work for.'

He took several moments to reply. Even then, he could only manage a, 'Why?'

'Because it's true.' She shrugged. 'Because I don't blame you for a being a good chef and leader.'

He narrowed his eyes. 'Sounds like you're implying something.'

'Why would I?' she asked sarcastically. 'It's not like I gave you a compliment, spoke highly and fairly about you to a potential employee, and you're choosing to focus on the negative in all that.'

All fair points and, consistent with his mood, that annoyed him. He bit down on his tongue. After a few seconds, she sighed.

'Look, I get that you're in competition mode, or whatever, but I'm not going to keep defending you for acting boorish. If you want Cherise to get to know you, you should show her who you are.

Unless, of course, you *are* boorish, and the man who was kind to me this morning and this entire time actually doesn't exist.'

She sounded tired, defeated, and his heart turned. But he couldn't tell her that he was going through something. How could he? He didn't understand it himself. It had to do with her, and with him not trusting himself around her, and that sounded like…like admitting that he was still the same fool who had let the people in his past take advantage of him.

'Yeah, I thought I might have been fooling myself,' she said softly. She closed her eyes before he could see any emotion. When she opened them again, they were unreadable. 'Cherise asked if we'd be interested in having a drink with her after work. I said yes, but now I'm not so sure.'

She turned on her heel. It took him a beat before he could move after her.

'You're not going to go?'

'No, I'm going.' She didn't stop walking when he fell into step beside her. 'I'm just not speaking for you. If you want to go, you can tell her yourself.'

It took him all of the way back to Cherise to decide that he would be going, too. In the mood he was in, heaven had better help him.

'You're not drinking?'

'Oh. Um…no.' Alexa had prepared for this in

the car. But there was something about actually being asked about her pregnancy, even indirectly, that made her freeze up. Probably the fact that she had to lie. 'I'm driving.'

'One drink wouldn't hurt,' Cherise said kindly.

There was nothing Alexa wanted less than kindness at that moment.

'She's a lightweight,' Benjamin cut in. 'One drink and she's about as tipsy as I am after four. So, to answer your question—one drink *would* hurt.'

If she went by Benjamin's tone, it wasn't kindness that inspired his words. But it wasn't malice either, and he was saving her from having to think about a more intricate lie. She gave him a half-smile in thanks, but looked away before she could see whether he smiled back. He was acting weird, and she didn't want to be hurt by whatever mood he was in.

Because you're already hurt.

No, she told the inner voice. She wasn't hurt by Benjamin's attitude. So what if he was acting like the old Benjamin? The one who was reluctant and competitive and reminded her more of her brother than of the person she was beginning to think of as more than an acquaintance?

If anything, the problem was that she had begun to think of him in a friendly manner. He wasn't her friend—she wouldn't make that mistake—but she'd confided in him and kissed him. No wonder she was feeling a little out of sorts now that he was acting like someone she hadn't confided in or kissed. She should have anticipated it, and she hadn't, and that was partly why she was feeling this way.

Benjamin had always been so competitive in class. She hadn't known him before, so she'd assumed he was just a competitive person. Working with her brother, stealing her head chef... Those things seemed to prove it. Then he'd pretended to be her boyfriend in front of Lee. She'd seen him with his mother, he'd offered to give her Cherise... Those things didn't seem like a person who was inherently competitive, but simply someone who liked competition.

There was nothing wrong with that. Hell, she was even willing to be in the competition with him. But that was before today had happened. Before she'd seen him watching her as she worked and she could all but feel the frustration radiating off him. He glanced at her so many times that she knew he was comparing. It was common sense as much as it was experience; she'd spent her entire childhood knowing what that comparison looked like. Lee had done it to her. And she had no desire, none, to be a basis of comparison again.

That was what this empty feeling in her chest was. Annoyance that Benjamin saw her as someone to beat. Someone to be better than. She didn't think better or worse had anything to do with Cherise's choice; it would be the person Cherise got along with best. Except it was clear Benjamin didn't see it that way. So she was annoyed. Maybe a little disappointed. But that was it.

'He's right,' she said with a quick smile. 'I've never been able to hold my alcohol well.'

'Fortunately we don't have that in common,' Cherise said, lifting the glass the bartender set in front of her. She downed it, hissing as she slammed the glass back on the counter. 'I can drink with the best of them.' She grinned. 'I probably shouldn't tell potential employers that.'

'Why not?' Benjamin asked. 'It's not likely we wouldn't find out.'

'I don't intend on drinking on the job. Or coming in hungover.'

'The longer you spend working with us, the higher the possibility of a fun night out. Or some kind of event.' Benjamin shrugged. 'We would have found out during the second or third drinking game of the night.'

'You play drinking games with your staff?'

Benjamin raised his glass and tilted it to her. 'We're not of the belief that there should be all work and no play.'

'That happens at Infinity, too, Alexa?'

'Oh, no,' Alexa said with a shake of her head. 'I let my employees have their fun on their own time. Making sure they have that time is more of a priority to me.'

'What about team morale?' Benjamin asked her.

'Created through good pay cheques and a healthy working environment.' She waited a beat. 'In the Rough should try it.'

'Ooh,' Cherise said with a smile. 'Harsh.'

'And probably undeserved.' Alexa smiled back, but didn't look at Benjamin.

'Probably?' he said.

She directed the smile at him, but it wasn't genuine. Nor was the teasing tone of his voice.

'You guys are really cute together,' Cherise said. 'You've never thought about one big business?'

'Oh, no,' she said at the same time Benjamin chuckled with a shake of his head.

'Why not?' Cherise asked. 'You're both skilled. Can you imagine what you could create together?'

'You're only saying this because we're both so wonderful and you'd rather not choose,' Alexa teased, trying to ease the tension that was settling in her stomach. 'If we joined forces you would be our second in command, and you're drunk on the prospect of such power.'

'Well, you're not wrong.'

They laughed. The tension unfurled. Then there was a tap on the microphone. They turned to a small stage at the opposite end of the room as a tall woman with tattoos up and down her arms cleared her throat.

'Thank you all for coming to Wild Acorn tonight.'

There were cheers from who Alexa assumed

were regulars. They sat at a table in the front, all still fairly formally dressed as though they'd come straight from work. She could see that happening. The bar was down a quiet road in Somerset West near the Institute, and they'd followed Cherise to get there. There was no way they would have found it by themselves, and yet it seemed popular.

'As most of you know, tonight is karaoke night—' she paused for another round of cheers '—and for those of you who don't, I thought I'd go over the rules.'

'There are rules for karaoke?' Alexa said under her breath.

'One,' the lady continued, seemingly answering Alexa, 'you have to take this seriously. No making anyone uncomfortable with a bad rendition of some famous ballad.' There was a beat. 'Just kidding! The only rule is that you have fun. Sing from the heart, dance if you will, and the best performer tonight has their tab taken care of.'

'Nice prize,' Benjamin commented. He looked at Cherise. 'Did you bring us here thinking you could make us sing?'

His smile faded when she answered, 'Hoping to.' She looked from Benjamin to Alexa. 'Who's going to go first?'

CHAPTER TWELVE

'I FEEL LIKE I shouldn't be watching this.' He was about to reply, but Cherise's voiced cracked on a high note and he winced instead. Alexa looked at him with a wrinkled nose. 'Yeah, we definitely shouldn't be watching this.'

'It's a bar. Where are we going to go?'

'You're saying we're trapped.' She took a long sip from her drink, studying Cherise as she executed some dance moves. 'I didn't think we would see how Cherise responds in a disaster at such an early stage.'

'And she responds—' he waited for Cherise to finish moonwalking '—poorly, apparently.'

Alexa gave a laugh. It wasn't the first time she'd done it that evening, but it sounded like her first genuine one. He couldn't be critical of it, of her, when he knew he was the reason she wasn't enjoying herself. And he felt terrible because of it.

With each sip of alcohol, he'd gained clarity. By the end of his second glass, he'd realised he was conflating his insecurities about trusting himself with his insecurities about trusting Alexa. He didn't know if she was fooling him; he didn't know if he could trust his gut when it told him she wasn't. His third glass told him he had been a jerk today, trying to figure it out. He started ordering water instead of alcohol, and was now wondering what the best way was to apologise.

'Look, Alexa—'

'Your turn!' she exclaimed, cutting him off.

He narrowed his eyes. 'I didn't say I was going to go up there.'

'You didn't say you weren't either.' She lifted a shoulder. 'I'm not the one asking you to go on stage.'

She tilted her head, gesturing to Cherise, who was eagerly waving at them.

'That wave could be for you, too.'

'It could,' she acknowledged, 'but since you're volunteering...'

'I'm not—'

In a movement quicker than he could have defended himself against, she stuck a hand underneath his arm and poked his armpit. Hard. The result was both surprise and amusement—he'd always been ticklish there. It was also a hand which popped into the sky, making it seem as though he were volunteering.

'Clever.' He stood, walked until he was so close to her he could smell the mint on her breath from her virgin mojito. 'But I'm clever, too.'

She tilted her head up, her eyes cool. 'Not everything is a competition.'

'No, it's not.' He lowered slightly, bringing their faces close. 'This isn't me competing. It's getting revenge.'

'Revenge?'

'You're going to do this with me.'

She smiled. It was mocking and unconcerned and—though he had no idea how or why—incredibly sexy.

'Oh, no, Benjamin, I will not be doing this with you.'

'Except—' he lifted a hand and tucked a stray curl behind her ear '—you are. Otherwise this would seem like a seduction to anyone looking.'

She pressed up on her toes, bringing their faces closer. 'Isn't it?'

'No.' It was though. And somehow he was being seduced, too. 'It's a request to do a duet.'

'I'm not doing a duet.'

'Not even for your fake boyfriend?'

Her lips parted. He brushed a thumb over it. When hot air touched his skin, he inhaled sharply. Then exhaled, because it felt as though he'd inhaled a copious amount of desire for her, too. His brain scrambled trying to remember what he'd intended when he stood up. To make it seem as if he was asking her to join him? To touch her and remind himself that she was the person she seemed to be, independent and not manipulative and certainly not who his fears made her out to be?

She took his hand, pulled it away from her face. 'This isn't going to happen.' The statement was ambiguous enough that it made him wonder what she was talking about until she clarified. 'I'm not making a fool of myself up there.'

He swallowed. Right. Of course she was talking about the singing and not…whatever had just happened.

'It'll be fun.'

'How?'

'We'll sing together. We'll both sing poorly together, I mean.'

'Yet another reason not to do it.'

'We're not auditioning for a singing competition,' he said, frustrated now. 'We're only singing.'

'No, I meant that if you sing badly, I refuse to sing with you.' She stood, emptying her glass as she did. 'I will not let my perfect soprano be tarnished by you.'

He couldn't even argue with that since he'd said he sang poorly. Then he realised she was moving to the stage, and he blinked. Why had she been arguing with him if she intended on singing? Was he really that awful that she didn't want to be on stage with him?

Yes, probably, he thought, sitting back down and offering Cherise a weak smile when she joined him. He'd been terrible to Alexa all day—

save for that morning. But that morning had felt as though they were in a bubble, and once things had got real, the bubble had popped and he...

He'd fallen hard to the ground while Alexa somehow stayed afloat, looking down at him in pity. Disappointment. Could he even blame her?

'I thought you were going to go up with her.'

'Me, too.'

'Your seduction didn't work?' Cherise gave him a sly grin. He smiled back weakly.

'Apparently not. I'm going to have to work on it.'

'Probably,' she said, bringing her beer to her lips. 'She doesn't seem like the type of person to fall for the usual stuff. She's tougher, but that kind of makes it mean more, in my opinion.'

He thought about it as he turned to the stage, watching as Alexa waited for the music to play. A couple of guys in the front were eyeing her in appreciation, and he had the absurd urge to get up and shield her from their view. But that made no sense, the desire less so, and instead he kept looking at Alexa.

She looked comfortable there, her clothing still strange, still chic. She'd tied her hair up again, but it was higher than it had been in the morning, piled onto the top of her head as if she'd put it there and forgotten about it. The waves refused to be tamed that way, though, and they fell over her forehead, created the shortest and strangest fringe he'd ever seen. It was also the cutest. Hell, she was cute. And sexy, and enticing, and he was pretty sure he had a problem.

Then she started to sing and he stopped thinking about that altogether.

Her voice was smooth and clear. Perfectly pitched on the higher notes; soulfully deep on the lower notes. She swayed in time to the beat, slowly, smiling when the lyrics were saucy or snarky.

'You've got to be kidding me,' Cherise said somewhere halfway into the song. 'She sings like it's what she does for a living.'

He agreed, but he was too enamoured to respond. He couldn't take his eyes off her, his ears thanked him profusely, and his mind was incredibly glad he hadn't spoiled this with his own voice, which was comparable to a cat's on a good day. When she was done, the entire room exploded with applause. Everyone was looking at her in appreciation now. She smiled brightly, happily, and he couldn't quite believe she was the same woman who could skin him and lay the spoils on the floor as she walked over them.

Damn if that brightness, that happiness didn't draw him in as much as her sharp wit.

'Stop looking at me like that,' Alexa said as soon as Cherise got into the taxi she'd called. Cherise was having her brother use her spare key to pick up her car, since she wasn't in any condition to drive. 'It's unnerving.'

'I just… I can't believe you've been hiding that voice away.'

'I wasn't hiding it away.' She hoped to heaven her skin wasn't glowing at the compliment the way her stupid heart was. 'It's never come up. Why would I bring it up?'

'Because it sounded like *that*?' He gestured with a thumb to the bar behind them. 'I'm still trying to figure out how you managed to do that.'

'Easy. I opened my mouth, and instead of speaking, I sang.'

'Like an angel.' She laughed. 'I'm not even mad you're being snarky,' he said, his voice filled with wonder. 'You should be singing.'

'Do you know,' she said after a moment, 'I'm really good at maths? I scored in the top five per cent of the province in my final year of school. I had a couple of bursaries to study maths that were generous.'

She didn't mention that her parents had applied for all those bursaries. They'd been so disappointed when she'd chosen not to take any of them that they hadn't even cared that she'd chosen business management instead. Well, they had cared. If they hadn't, she would have gone to culinary school from the beginning.

'Congratulations?' Benjamin's voice interrupted her thoughts.

She laughed. 'My point is that just because I'm good at something doesn't mean I want to do it for a living. I love what I do. I love the challenge of running a restaurant. I love working with my chefs to make efficient meals that are delicious and new and…' She broke off, feeling heat spread over her cheeks. 'Anyway. I won't be leaving to sing any time soon.'

'A pity,' he said with a small smile. 'But I suppose, since you're good at running a business, too, the world isn't completely missing out on your talents.'

Somehow, it didn't feel like a compliment.

'I should get going. The ride back home is long.'

'Yeah.'

But he didn't let her pass him, and, since he was standing in front of her, she kind of needed him to.

'Benjamin—'

'Is there anything you aren't good at?'

And there it was.

There isn't one thing you're bad at. Nothing. You do everything well. It's annoying.

Exhausting, too, she'd wanted to tell her brother. She wouldn't call it lucky that she was good at the things her parents thought she should be good at. It was half luck, half hard work, and all exhaustion. Her parents had come to expect her to be good at everything, so she didn't think she could fail. If she did, they would care for her even less than they already did. As a kid, she couldn't bear the thought of it.

That was the one thing she wasn't good at: accepting that her family wasn't what she wanted them to be. She tried and tried to make her parents proud, but nothing she did would ever be enough. She had tried with Lee, too, because he was the only one who would understand how their parents' pressure could become unbearable. But he'd had no interest. For every outreached hand was a slap in the form of a record she'd set that he'd broken, or a mark of hers that he'd beaten. When he'd bought the building out from under her she'd finally decided to stop reaching out her hand, and hoped it would mean no more slapping.

Except it still came. And apparently through proxies now, too.

'I should really get home.'

She moved past him but he caught her wrist. She looked at him.

'You're not going to answer?'

'What would you like me to say?' She was proud of the stiffness in her voice. It meant the thickness in her throat hadn't tainted her speaking. 'Yes, I'm good at everything. Except making rational decisions, like when I pretended you were my boyfriend. If I hadn't, we wouldn't be in this position. I wouldn't be in this position.'

He frowned, and let go of her arm. 'I'm sorry. I didn't mean to...' He exhaled. 'I'm sorry,' he said again.

'Okay.' She swallowed. 'Now can I leave?'

CHAPTER THIRTEEN

HE WANTED TO say sorry. For acting like a jerk the day before; for making those assumptions the night before. He arrived at the Institute early in the hope of finding a moment to talk with her again before the course started. No such luck. Which wasn't a problem—until the start of the class came and both Alexa and Cherise weren't there. Cherise rushed in ten minutes late, looking like hell.

'Sorry,' she muttered. 'My car broke down on the way. And I probably drank too much last night, made a fool of myself, and I promise you it won't happen again.'

'Sorry to hear about the car,' he said. 'About last night... You don't have to apologise. You're not working for us yet.'

'But I would like to, and I seem to have handed you reasons not to hire me.'

He smiled. 'It's nice to know you actually want this.'

'I really do.' She smiled, but it faded almost immediately. 'Although I think I spoilt my chances with Alexa. I'm pretty sure I'm the reason she's sick.'

'She's sick?'

'Yeah.' She gave him a strange look. 'She didn't tell you?'

'No.' When he realised why she was so surprised, he cleared his throat. 'We're supposed to have a date after this today. I think maybe she didn't want to tell me in case I cancelled.'

'Oh, that's so sweet,' Cherise said. 'You guys are cute.'

'Thanks.'

They fell into silence as the instructor began to guide them in a brand-new decorating nightmare. He couldn't really focus. He was too busy thinking about Alexa. He stumbled his way through the class, but that was pretty usual for him. He did notice that Cherise's hangover, and the rough morning she'd had, hadn't affected her concentration. She did the work perfectly, patiently, without one mistake. Which told him she wouldn't bring personal problems into the workplace. He was almost thankful for the night they'd had before.

She seemed forgiving of his lack of decorating skills, and by the end of it he knew their one-on-one time had done wonders for their professional working relationship. He even suspected that he might have had an edge over Alexa. It made him feel guilty. Not that he had any reason to feel guilty. He hadn't orchestrated her sickness, had he? He hadn't done anything so that he could spend time with Cherise while Alexa stayed home, sick, probably unable to breathe, her nose blocked, chest phlegmy...

He grunted, got into his car, and started it. Then he grunted again, because he already knew where he was going to, even before he started driving to the pharmacy. When he got there, he started grabbing things that usually helped him when he was feeling under the weather. He walked past an aisle, paused, looked down it. Saw a bunch of pregnancy and maternity things. Vitamins, baby bottles. He looked at the things in his hands. She probably couldn't use any of this, being pregnant. He went back to the pharmacist, and got fewer things. Bought ingredients to make some good chicken soup. Some fresh bread, too.

None of that made it easier when he was finally in front of her door. He felt as though he was intruding on her space. She obviously didn't want him to know she was sick, or she would have told him. Now he was pitching up at her door, assuming that she wanted to see him? Especially after how he'd treated her the day before?

He took a deep breath and was brutally honest with himself. He'd told himself guilt was the reason he was there. Maybe it was, but not only because he got to spend time with Cherise when

Alexa couldn't. No, it was redemption. For how he had treated her the day before. To ease his conscience, or to make it up to her, he didn't know. Either way, he was there, and he was going to make sure she knew he wasn't all bad.

He knocked on the door. Again when he heard nothing inside. A long while later, he heard some shuffling. Then the door opened. He almost dropped everything in his hands.

'You're, um…you're…' He cleared his throat. He couldn't…point out what the problem was without telling her that he had looked at her chest. But not pointing it out meant he studiously had to avoid looking down. He gritted his teeth, then thought it might look intimidating and offered her a smile. 'You're okay,' he finished lamely.

She folded her arms. Doing so should have covered the flesh spilling out of the top of the loose nightgown she wore. Instead, because of the sheer generosity of her breasts, the movement pushed them together instead.

'What are you doing here?'

'I heard you're sick.'

'Yes.'

He frowned. 'I was sorry to hear that.'

'Thank you.'

He gestured to the bags in his hands. 'Do you think I could come in?'

'Why?'

'I…' Was he really this bad at showing he cared

about something? 'I thought I'd make you some soup.'

She studied him, expression unreadable, though there were dark rings around her eyes. Seconds later, as if she knew he'd seen it, she sagged against the doorframe. 'It's a bad bout of nausea. I thought because things weren't so bad in my first trimester—' She shrugged. 'Apparently my babies hate me.'

'They don't hate you,' he said automatically.

'I appreciate that.' She exhaled slowly. 'You can come in. But you can't cook anything. I'm pretty sure I'd throw up if you did.' She cast a look at him. 'That's not a reflection on your cooking or anything.'

'Thanks,' he said dryly.

He followed her inside, closing the door behind him. He wasn't sure what to do now that his grand plan wouldn't work. Plus, seeing her like this was a distraction. She'd gone back to the sofa, curled up and closed her eyes, as if he weren't in her space. And he shouldn't have been.

There wasn't much he could do about morning sickness. With a cold or flu he could ply her with medication, encourage her to sleep. But constant nausea? Enough that she couldn't come in to work? What was he supposed to do about that?

Since she wasn't looking, he asked the internet that question. Then he wandered into her kitchen, set down the things he'd bought, and looked in her cupboards. They were meticulously packed. He couldn't see what order they were in, but they were definitely in order. Same with the fridge. He tried not to disturb anything as he looked for what the internet suggested. Minutes later, he walked into the kitchen, set the tea on the coffee table and crouched down in front of her.

'Alexa?' She opened one eye. Somehow, she managed a glare with it. He resisted his smile. 'Have you eaten anything today?'

'Some toast this morning.'

'This morning?'

'I haven't really had the energy for much.'

'Okay.' He frowned. 'Well, the internet said something bland would do you good.'

'Sounds amazing.'

He chuckled softly. 'How about some brown rice? Plain avocado? Or toast with peanut butter and banana? Broth?'

Her other eye opened. 'Sounds like you're trying to get nutrients into me.'

'They said it would be best if what you ate had nutrients in it.'

'They?'

He scratched the back of his head when his skin began to prickle with heat. 'The internet.'

'You went on the internet for this?'

'Did any of what I offered sound appealing to you?' he asked instead of answering.

'The toast,' she replied after a moment. 'It's

not the most appealing, but it's the easiest option, which we'll both be grateful for if I end up throwing it up.'

He appreciated her logic, but he would actually feel better if he could put some more effort into whatever he made her. To assuage the guilt, he told himself. For redemption, he added. Not because he cared enough to put more effort into it.

'On it. Also, I made you some ginger tea.'

'Did the internet tell you to do that?' She was teasing him, giving him a small smile to show it.

He offered her a hand. 'If you want me to help you sit up, you won't get the answer to that.'

'It would almost be worth it.'

But she took his hand and he helped her up. Her colour didn't look good, but that made sense since she was nauseous and hadn't eaten since the morning. He handed her the tea. Her fingers brushed his as she did, and for some bizarre reason a shiver went through him. Bizarre, because things were weird with them, and she was sick, and the only reason he was in her flat was because he felt guilty. He shouldn't feel attraction in this moment—or whatever it was that caused that shiver. It also had nothing to do with her cleavage, impressive and visible as it was. It was simply her, and how much she intrigued and confused him.

He exhaled, leaving her to the tea as he went to make her toast. It was quick work. When he handed it to her, he thought he'd head back to the kitchen, start making a broth even though she didn't seem to want it. But she said, 'Wait.'

He turned. 'Yeah?'

'You didn't make yourself anything?'

His mouth curved. 'Did I make myself some peanut butter and banana toast as well? No. Surprisingly.'

'No need to be smug about your ability to eat something other than this.' But her eyes were warm. 'Thank you.'

'You don't have to thank me.'

'Why not?'

She tore a small piece off the toast and put it into her mouth, looking at him expectantly.

'Oh…er… It wasn't a big deal.'

She chewed and finished. Swallowed. 'It is to me.'

There was a brief moment where they stared at one another before he realised he'd better look away if he wanted to keep his sanity. Although deep down he knew it wasn't his sanity he was worried about.

'Will you sit down?' she asked, looking down now, too.

'Do you want me to?'

'I wouldn't have asked if I didn't want you to.'

'Good point.' He smiled at the dry tone. 'I'll just grab myself something to drink.'

'Yeah, of course. Anything in the fridge is yours.'

He went to the kitchen, got himself a sparkling

water, and went back to the lounge. It didn't even occur to him to dawdle, or delay long enough that she would be done with her meal. The opposite, in fact. He wanted to sit with her, talk to her, and he didn't know what it meant.

Or he did, but he preferred not to think about it.

When he got back, he saw her toast looked the same as it had when he left.

'Feel sick?'

'Not at the moment. I'm waiting to see how my stomach's going to react to it.' She took a slice of banana off the toast and ate it. 'It seems cruel to me that someone who enjoys food as much as I do can't eat it.'

'But it hasn't been like this your entire pregnancy, you said?'

'No, it hasn't. I have been nauseous, but it's been pretty consistently in the mornings before work and the evenings after. I thought I was lucky.' She groaned. 'Turns out my body was lulling me into a false sense of security.'

'How has today been different?'

'You mean apart from the waves of nausea all day?' She tore off another piece of toast, but didn't eat it. Instead, she patted the seat next to her. He didn't even hesitate. Just obeyed. 'I've been throwing up more, though that seems consistent with being nauseous more, doesn't it? I've also been a little dizzier, but that could be because I haven't been eating.'

'You should have been.'

'I know,' she agreed, easily enough that he knew she wasn't feeling herself. 'But it seemed like a lot of energy to go to the kitchen and get something to eat when I could lie here.'

He studied her. Took a long drink of his water to make sure he really wanted to say what he thought he wanted to say. Sighed.

'Look, you can argue with me when you have energy for it later, okay?'

Her eyebrows rose. 'A promising start to a conversation.'

'It's concern.' He paused. 'You have to look after yourself, Alexa. That's how you're looking after your babies right now. By looking after yourself.'

Her hand went to her belly, before she brought it back to the toast. She put a piece in her mouth, then opened her palm as if to agree with him. Something in the gesture made her seem so vulnerable, he wanted to pull her into his arms and comfort her. Hell, there was a part of him that wanted to do that regardless of the vulnerability.

He settled for edging closer to her.

She deserved to have people to care about her. She deserved that she care about herself, which he thought she might struggle with. He had no proof, and he wouldn't dare ask, since he was already pushing his luck with their current conversation. But something about Alexa made him think that she put others ahead of herself. Even with her pregnancy. She was trying so hard to make things with Cherise work. Not for herself, he thought, but for her restaurant.

Part of that was because Lee had taught her she couldn't let her guard down. And yes, when he'd offered Victor Fourie that job, he'd shown her that, too. Now she was terrified of going on leave because she thought it would put all she'd worked for in jeopardy.

Someone who'd grown up as she had would hate that idea. They'd hate that it might result in failure, too. He couldn't imagine how much that would mess with someone's mind. He could, however, see that he'd contributed to her fears. That his question the night before, about her being good at everything, would add to that pressure. Which would explain how tense she'd got.

He would apologise for it. Not now. Now he had a different mission.

'You're going to have to take care of yourself when they're here, too,' he said quietly. 'It's the most important thing, your health. Not only because they need you to be healthy to take care of them.'

'What else is there?'

'Your happiness. It's going to be important to them. They'll want to see you living your life as you would have even if they weren't there. That means taking care of yourself, making sure you're as important in your life as they are.'

'You speak as if you know.'

'I...do.'

It felt a little like a betrayal, admitting that. But if he had to betray his mother—just a little—to make Alexa see she was as important as her children, then so be it. Hell, he reckoned his mother might even agree. She'd called him two days after that dinner with Alexa and told him she liked his new girlfriend.

'The baby situation is complicated,' Nina had said, 'but I can see why you couldn't move on without giving things with her a try. She's refreshing.'

'You're good at it,' Alexa said, piercing through the haze of memories.

'What?'

'Caring for people.'

The words hit him in the gut. 'I've had a lot of practice.'

'With your mom? Inference,' she said when he looked at her.

'I wouldn't say I took care of her.'

'I didn't say that you did. Only that you cared for her.'

He almost laughed at how she'd caught him out. He didn't because it wasn't funny.

'She needed a lot of support with the fibromyalgia.'

'Support can sometimes mean caring for them.'

'That's not what happened with my mom,' he said tersely.

'It was a compliment, Benjamin.' Her expression was a combination of bewilderment, kindness, and…hurt? Had he hurt her? But then she clarified. 'Speaking as someone who didn't have it all that much in her life, it's certainly a compliment.'

'I'm sorry.' He stared at the bottle in his hand. 'I seem to be apologising a lot to you these days.'

She shrugged. 'It's because I rub you up the wrong way. What?' she asked with a little laugh. 'You don't think I noticed? It's kind of hard not to.'

'To be fair, I think the reverse applies, too, and yet you don't seem to apologise nearly as often as I do.'

'I'm more irreverent.' She gave him a half-smile. 'I'm definitely less in touch with my emotions. I find them—' she wrinkled her nose '—inconvenient.'

He laughed, and some of the tension in his stomach dissipated. 'I'm not much more in touch with my emotions. They're inconvenient as hell, and it's easier to ignore them.'

'The apologies tell me you don't do the easier thing,' she pointed out. 'You might not be able to deal with them very well, but you feel them. It's more than I can say for myself.'

'And why's that?'

She heaved out a sigh. 'I don't know. No, no, I do,' she interrupted herself. 'Honestly, it's just… I guess ignoring them is what I'm used to. If I had felt every little thing when I was a kid, I wouldn't function nearly as well as I do today.'

She began to eat again, slowly, and he waited until she was done to ask the questions tumbling into his head. When she was done, she set down the remaining toast on the table. Then she moved closer to him. His heart thudded, but she didn't do anything else. Not one more thing, even though his body felt as if it was bracing for impact.

'Do you want to talk about it?' he asked hoarsely.

'I don't think so.' Her expression was uncertain when she met his eyes. 'Is that okay?'

'Of course. We don't have to talk about anything you don't want to.'

'I will, someday. It seems like a lot of effort to think about it now.'

She rested her head on his shoulder. He froze—but not for long. Slowly, so he wouldn't spook her, he lifted his arm. She immediately snuggled into his chest.

It was a good thing he was sitting, or the way his knees had gone weak would have taken him to the ground.

'Tell me what your day was like?' she asked. 'Was Cherise as hungover as she should have been after last night?'

Somehow, he managed to laugh. But as he told her about his day, it felt more natural, them sitting like this, talking. He was honest about how things had gone with Cherise, and she didn't seem upset about it. She asked him questions, laughed at his description of how terribly he'd done. He kept talking when she shifted onto her side, curling into much the same position he'd found her in. Except now she was curled into his side, then lying with her head on his lap. When she faltered he lowered his voice but kept talking, since it seemed to soothe her.

She was fast asleep shortly after, but he didn't get up as he should have. He stroked her hair, which was messy and somehow beautiful. He brushed her skin, bronze and smooth. He sat there, her warmth comforting something inside him. Much too long later, he took the dishes to the kitchen and began making her something to eat for when she got up. When he was done with that, he let himself out, but not without one last look in her direction.

She looked so peaceful, lying under the blanket he'd covered her with. His heart did something in his chest. Lurched, turned over, filled—he wasn't sure of the description. He only knew that seeing her, speaking her with her, caring for her...

It had changed him. Something had changed between them, too. He wondered if she would acknowledge it. He wondered if he would.

CHAPTER FOURTEEN

SHE WAS FEELING better the next day. She hadn't thrown up the toast Benjamin made her, and she'd slept through the entire night. It didn't seem normal to feel better when the day before she'd basically been knocked out. She supposed that was pregnancy. Or she hoped it was. If it wasn't, everyone in class, including her, was going to get more than they'd bargained for.

She had a nice long shower, got dressed, and went to the kitchen. Everything was in its place; it was as if Benjamin hadn't been there. And maybe he hadn't been. It seemed consistent with the state she'd been in the day before. Maybe she'd conjured him up, and he hadn't been sweet and patient and caring. He hadn't made her laugh, held her, stayed with her until she'd fallen asleep.

Except when she opened her fridge she found a glass container with clear broth in it and a sticky note—she had no idea where he'd found one.

In case you're feeling up to it. B.

B. B was definitely Benjamin. She couldn't deny that he'd been there any more. Him leaving food for her meant she hadn't imagined he was sweet and patient and caring either. And if that was true, she had to believe that he'd made her laugh, held her, stayed with her as she'd fallen asleep. And he'd cooked. For her.

She took a long, deep breath as she removed the broth from the fridge and heated it up. But it didn't help, and she spent the entire time eating the flavourful liquid quietly sobbing. She was certain it was pregnancy hormones. Mostly. She supposed that was the problem.

But when was the last time someone in her life had checked on her when she was ill? When was the last time she'd let someone in her life do that?

Kenya would have, if Alexa let her. She had, once upon a time. When Kenya had started working at Infinity, something had clicked between them and they'd got along well. But Alexa had confined that relationship to the restaurant. She'd thought it best, easier, better for the restaurant. Now, after the entire Benjamin debacle, Alexa wondered if it was simply better for *her*. If she didn't go out with Kenya, she wouldn't risk getting hurt. Except by doing that, she'd hurt Kenya. And that, by some cruel twist of fate, had hurt her, too.

She thought about it the entire drive to the Institute. Once she got there, she made sure there wasn't a trace of her crying on her face. She had a feeling Benjamin would pounce on it if he saw it. Which turned out to be a fruitless concern anyway, since he wasn't there.

'He must have what you had,' Cherise said with a knowing look. Alexa murmured in agreement. She had no choice but to. She'd told Cherise she had a twenty-four-hour bug, which seemed like a half-truth. But she knew that what she had wasn't contagious. She also knew Benjamin well enough that she could piece together what had happened.

When he'd told her about his day the night before, he'd been excited, but restrained. That restraint had come through most strongly when he was relaying the more fun parts of the day, as if he'd felt bad. The fact that he wasn't here told her he did feel bad. It made her think the reason he was at her place last night had been because he'd felt bad, too.

She set it aside as she spent the day with Cherise. At one point, her prospective chef pointed out something Alexa was doing poorly. Alexa thanked Cherise, adjusted, and realised that, while it had helped in some ways, it hadn't in others. So she coached Cherise through doing it her way, and Cherise was pleased with the ending.

'Maybe we can put it together and come up with a technique that could give us the best of both worlds.'

'Yeah, that would be great,' Cherise said with a bright smile.

She smiled back, and wondered if Benjamin had felt the same glow of appreciation at connecting with Cherise. Her heart skipped at the thought. Not at its content, but that she'd thought it at all. That she'd thought about him at all. It was dangerous; more so because the thoughts were accompanied by a soft, squishy feeling in her chest that she had no name for but made her feel warm and safe.

But how could she feel safe when even feeling that told her she was in danger? It was a conundrum, one she made no effort to clarify, even when she told herself to. She set it aside again, tried to focus on the day with Cherise. She felt worn at the end of it, her legs aching and her back, too, although it was much too early for her to be feeling that way. Then again, those were normal, non-pregnancy feelings after a long day. Today had seemed long, despite the fact that it was shorter than most days for her. Maybe being pregnant meant the length of what was long would change.

It didn't bode well for all she had to do before she went on maternity leave. Or should she even go on leave at all? She'd thought it would be a good idea to get to know her babies, but now it felt as if she was leaving her first baby, her restaurant, exposed. It was her responsibility to make sure it wasn't exposed. The fact that she hadn't meant that she'd...failed.

She drove home with that troubling thought

racing in her mind. When she stopped, though, she didn't find herself at her home, but at In the Rough. It was the first time she'd been there since Lee had bought the building. She'd refused to go, on principle, despite her parents calling her stubborn. But the day that she'd wanted to show them her building, and they'd told Lee about it, had changed things for her. Their disappointment no longer hurt as much as it had. Or maybe it did hurt, but it didn't cripple her any more.

She still tried with them: a phone call every couple of weeks, a dinner once a month, telling them important news. But the truth was that she didn't want them in her life as much any more. Especially when they insisted on having Lee be part of the package.

Slowly, she climbed out of the car, staring up at the sign as she did. Black lettering flickered at her against the brick façade, courtesy of a faint white light outlining the letters. The front of the restaurant itself was all glass, allowing her to see the patrons laughing and enjoying themselves.

She took a breath and walked into the restaurant. She took in the dark wooden feel of the place, noted the red-haired barperson. It was a strange experience, seeing the place done, compared to the last time she'd been there. More so comparing it to the vision of what she'd had for the space. She'd executed the idea almost identically at Infinity, but she'd had to make adjustments because it didn't fit as well in her current space as it would have there.

The disappointment of it washed over her, and she took another breath, deeper this time, before she walked to the bar.

'Do you know where I can find Benjamin?'

The woman quirked her brow. 'Who are you?'

'Oh. I'm…er…'

She didn't know what Benjamin had told his people. Of course, she knew what Lee knew, but that didn't mean he'd announced it to his entire staff. If he hadn't, she didn't want to complicate things by telling his employee she was his girl-friend. But she also didn't want him to know she was there. He'd likely pull a runner, pretend he was really sick, and she couldn't tell him he was being a jerk.

'Is he here?'

'He might be.' She tilted her head. 'You look familiar.'

'I don't think so.'

'No, you do.' The woman came closer, limping slightly as she did. 'Have you been here before?'

'Definitely not.' She tried to cover it up when she realised how that sounded. 'I mean, I haven't had the chance.'

'You're missing out.'

She took a look at the full restaurant. It was barely six in the evening and already the vibe was jovial. The patrons were pretty much as she had imagined when she'd thought about the space. Benjamin had clearly turned it into *the* place though, since it was just about bouncing with energy.

She turned back to the barperson. 'Apparently so.'

'I think, considering it's you and considering you're my main competition, that's almost a compliment.'

She was rolling her eyes before she was even facing him fully.

'Hi.'

'Hi.'

She wasn't prepared for the way he leaned in to her, or the kiss he brushed on her cheek. It wasn't a sensual greeting in theory, but the heat of it seared through her body.

'You're feeling better?'

'Much.' She started to brush her hair off her forehead, but stopped. The movement would make her look nervous. She was already feeling it; she didn't have to look it. 'Thanks for leaving me that broth.'

'Was it good?'

'You know it was,' she said with a half-smile. 'Stop looking for compliments.'

'You gave me one now, I think,' he replied with a half-smile of his own. 'But I won't push you to see if you have any more.'

'Good. You might not like what you find.'

'Mia, could you have a whiskey and—' He looked at her expectantly.

'Oh. Water.'

'And a water sent to my office, please?'

'Sure.'

Mia waved them off, but not before Alexa saw the questioning look in her eyes. Alexa couldn't blame her. A random woman comes to the bar, asking about the boss without giving any reason, and moments later the boss appears and whisks said woman into his office? It looked dodgy, even to her, and *she* was the random woman.

'Please, sit,' Benjamin said when they walked into the small space of his office.

'Thanks.'

She took the seat opposite him. The space was confined, making it big enough only for his desk, two chairs, and a cabinet.

'If you get a smaller desk, have some floating shelves installed, you could create more space for yourself.'

'Why would I want to?' he asked dryly. 'I have everything I need.'

'You're right.'

Purposefully, she swung her handbag to her lap. It knocked a pile of books off his desk. She gave him a look, then bent to pick the books up and set them back where they were.

'Why would you need more space?'

'Fine, you've proved your point.'

He was chuckling when a young man, probably early twenties, knocked on the door and set their drinks in front of them.

'Anything else?' he asked, after Benjamin thanked him.

'We're good for now,' Benjamin replied, looking at her to confirm. She nodded. 'I'll call the kitchen if I need anything else.' He waited until the man left. 'You would have had a smaller desk and floating shelves, wouldn't you?'

'Yeah. I was going to do the shelves on that wall.' She pointed at one wall. 'Put the desk here.' She pointed at the opposite wall. 'I probably would have got some fancy desk, with three sections that were stacked on top of one another, so I could have options to stand and have plenty of space.' She shrugged. 'I didn't need to in the end, because my current office is huge.'

'Rub it in, won't you?' But his eyes were serious. 'You really wanted this, didn't you?'

'I was going to buy it,' she said in answer. 'I had plans for it.' She picked up her water and took a sip to quench her suddenly dry throat. 'It taught me to act first, dream later. An important lesson.'

There was a long silence. She resisted the urge to fidget during it.

'He just bought this from under you?' Benjamin asked.

'Yes.'

'Knowing you wanted it?'

'Yes.'

Another pause.

'Then he offered the space to me.'

'He's smart.'

Seconds passed.

'He was using me.'

'Weren't you using him, too?'

'I don't feel like it's the same.'

'Probably not,' she conceded. 'Don't look so sad.' Sadness wasn't quite the emotion in his expression, but she went with it because it also wasn't *not* sadness. 'It turned out well in the end.'

'Yeah, but it's still…' He offered her a small smile. 'It's hard to wrap my head around. The man who gave me a chance did so by robbing you of something. I considered Lee to be a friend, and now I'm wondering whether I was a fool to do so.'

She thought about it. Sighed.

'This wasn't what I thought I'd be doing here, but okay.' She set her glass down. 'The Lee you know is the Lee you know. You've known him for years. You've worked with him. Have likely been through a lot with him. The way he's treated me doesn't change that.'

'It does though,' he said softly. 'He has the capacity to be cruel and—'

'Only with me,' she interrupted. 'It's part of why my parents could never understand why I had such a problem with him. They couldn't believe he was the person I was claiming he was, even though they created the environment that forced us to compete.'

'Forced…compete?' He leaned forward. 'What do you mean?'

She couldn't answer him. It would rip off the bandage that she had put over the wounds of her childhood. She'd spent her entire adult life trying to put, to keep, that bandage in place. She wouldn't remove it now because this man was asking her to.

'You, um… You don't look sick.'

He blinked. Seemingly acknowledged she didn't want to talk about it because he didn't press. Instead he leaned back in his chair.

'I am.' He gave a very fake cough.

She rolled her eyes, but smiled. 'You're obviously not. You didn't have to do that.'

'I didn't do anything.'

'Benjamin.'

He frowned. 'Fine. But I was only making sure the playing field was level.'

'Were you?' She bit her lip as she sat back. 'Was that what last night was, too? You were making sure things were level as you spent the night with me?'

'It wasn't quite spending the night,' he protested, colour lighting his cheeks.

'Of course not.' She didn't bother hiding her smile. 'But it was guilt, wasn't it? You felt guilty about getting a day with Cherise, and you came to look after me so you could tell yourself that you tried to make things better.'

'It wasn't exactly like that.'

She lifted her brows, waiting for him to tell her what it was like. He sighed impatiently.

'Maybe there was some guilt. But it was more because I wanted to apologise for being a brute the day before yesterday.'

'What was today, then?' she asked. 'Surely you made up for it last night? More than, even. You didn't have to do it.'

'It was fair.'

'It was stupid.'

'Can you just…?' He stopped, lowering his voice when the words came out loudly. 'Can you just say thank you?'

'No,' she said after a moment. 'I'm not going to thank you for feeling sorry for me.'

She stood, knocking over the books with her handbag again, this time unintentionally. With a sigh, she lowered to pick them up. Then found that she was stuck.

'Oh.'

'Oh.' He stood now, too. 'Oh, what?'

She tried with all her might to push up, but her balance was shot. It only ended up pushing her forward. She put a hand out in time to keep from knocking her head.

'Lex, are you okay? Are you in labour?'

'Of course I'm not in labour.' She scowled.

'I'm thirteen weeks pregnant. Of course I'm not in labour.'

'Okay.' He crouched down in front of her. 'Why are you not getting up, then?'

'Because—' she gritted her teeth '—I can't.'

'You can't get up?'

'Seems you need your core to stand up. Who knew?'

She could almost feel him laughing at her. She chose to ignore it. Largely because she really couldn't get up and the floor was surprisingly terrible to be on.

'Are you going to help me?'

'Yeah.' But she heard the click of a camera. Her head shot up.

'What did you do?'

'Nothing,' he said innocently, taking her under the arms and lifting her gently.

'Benjamin, if you took a photo of me struggling to get up, I swear I'll make you regret it.'

'Which is exactly why I need the photo. For protection.'

'Why do you need protection?'

'You're a voracious opponent.'

'Am I an opponent?' she asked lightly, though she didn't feel light. It had nothing to do with him taking a picture of her or getting stuck on the floor.

'I didn't mean it that way.'

'How did you mean it?'

'You're a sparring partner,' he said, shoving his hands into his jeans pockets. They were close enough that she could reach out and pull them out if she wanted to. 'We argue and debate. It's what we do.'

'Yeah, but all of that started because you saw me as an opponent *in that way*.' She lifted her head because, although it smarted, he was taller than her, and the lack of distance between them meant she had to. 'Something about me in class made you think of me as competition.'

'You were the best, Alexa.' He shrugged. 'People don't compete against someone in the middle. They do so with the person at the top. And you were.'

Or they compete with the only person who's there, she thought, remembering all the years her parents had encouraged her and Lee to be better than those around them. Their words weren't only for her and Lee; *they* competed with those around them, too. Even with one another. It seemed to invigorate their marriage though, rather than cause the relationship to crumble. Sometimes Alexa wondered whether she was their child, since she was the only one in the family who hadn't been invigorated by competition. She was the odd one out. Lee had simply been following their parents' example.

It didn't make it right though. At least not for her.

'I should… I should go.'

'Alexa,' he said, reaching for her hand. She stilled when he threaded their fingers together. Let herself go to him when he pulled her in. 'I didn't mean to upset you.'

'I know.'

'But you're upset.'

She sighed. 'It's not you. Well, not you alone.' When he only looked at her, the heat of his hand pulsing into her body, landing at her heart, she sighed again. 'I spent my entire life being the person Lee had to beat. Not because I was the best, or at the top, but because I was there. My parents told us to be the best. We got rewarded with love or gifts if we were.' She closed her eyes. 'I don't… I don't want to live my entire life like that. That's why I cut Lee out of it. That's why I barely speak to my parents.'

She dropped her head. It found a soft landing, and she realised he'd moved closer so she could lean against his chest. As it had the night before, it comforted her.

'This entire thing with Cherise is a nightmare for me,' she whispered. 'I just want it to be over. And before you say it—no, it won't be if you step back.'

'It will.'

She looked up at him. 'No, it won't. If you don't fight fairly, I'll know. More significantly, Lee will know. And he'll stop at nothing to convince Cherise to work for In the Rough, which will put me right back in the position I was in in the first place.'

She lifted a free hand and set it on his chest. Curled her fingers.

'You'll know, too. You'll know that you sacrificed this for me. I don't want that.' She beat her fist lightly against his chest. 'I want you to think of what's best for you. Fighting for this is what's best for you,' she clarified when he frowned.

His hand lifted, curled over her fist. 'I thought you didn't want us to compete.'

'I don't. But I'm not naïve enough to believe I won't encounter competition in my life. In my business. Just…' She sighed. 'Just make it a good one so we can all move forward without this haunting us.'

For some reason, she slid an arm around his waist, rested her head against his chest again. Her other hand remained in his as if they were about to dance.

'I'll be fine without you helping me, Ben. I promise.'

CHAPTER FIFTEEN

HE WANTED TO believe her. He really did. But how many times had his mother said she was fine, only for him to find her curled up in pain somewhere? He was tired of the people he cared about hurting. And damn it, he cared about Alexa. No matter how much he tried to use guilt, or logic, or whatever other reason he'd used in the last weeks as an excuse to see her and spend time with her. He cared about her. He wanted her to be okay. Whether that meant her health, or her restaurant.

He needed her to be okay.

The urgency of it was partly from an unknown source, partly from that caring. Hell, it was partly because she was standing in his arms, looking up at him with reassurance in her eyes. Her stomach was pressed into his, and the rounding of it—not much, but enough—sent a rush of protectiveness through him.

Feeling the rest of her body against his wasn't as harmless.

She wore another loose top, but it clung to her

breasts if nothing else, as if as amazed by them as he was. He hadn't been as fascinated by this part of the body since he was a teenager discovering his sexuality. His conclusion then had been that their biological function was as important as their appearance. He'd clearly been desperate to separate himself from his physical feelings then, which was most likely a form of protection. If he wasn't into romantic relationships, he would still be able to help at home.

His opinion had somewhat changed over the years. Probably because he'd learnt how to balance things better. If he prioritised, he could enjoy his physical feelings, too. He didn't have to shun them.

Thank goodness, or he might not have appreciated Alexa's breasts in that moment. And appreciating it caused his breath to go from simply oxygenating his body to giving her a signal something had changed. Her eyes fluttered up; something on his face had them clouding with desire. Most likely his own desire, his more rapid breathing.

He could appreciate more than Alexa's breasts though. Those eyes, clouded as they were, made him feel as though he were sitting in front of a fire on a rainy day. When they sparred, her gaze handed him a glass of whiskey, warming him from the inside, too. Her lips parted, and he couldn't resist dipping his head—until he realised what he was about to do.

'I'd like to kiss you,' he whispered.

'Okay,' she whispered back. 'Do it.'

'I was asking.'

'Your hand has been pressed into the small of my back for the better part of five minutes. Seconds ago was the first time you used it to pull me in closer. Now you want to ask?'

'I did?' He had no recollection of it. 'I'm sorry. I should have—'

He broke off when she put a finger over his lips. 'You weren't doing it on purpose. I understood that. It was part of the reason I didn't knee you in the groin.'

He laughed. 'If I ever do anything that makes you uncomfortable on purpose, please feel free to do just that.'

'I didn't need your permission.' Her mouth curved up. 'But thank you, I suppose. Now, shall we get back to that kissing thing?'

He kissed her then, glad she wasn't playing games when his need seemed to consume him. He moaned in relief when their lips touched and he felt the softness of her. Their essences tangled, their souls embraced, and he would never get over the enormity of it—from just a kiss.

Her tongue slipped between his lips, and he opened for her as desire pulsed inside him. She tasted sweet—or was that the promise of her? The idea of what they could share if they ever allowed this feeling to become more than a stolen moment. It didn't matter. All that did was his heart thumping harder against his breastbone, almost as though it were hard work; almost as though there were water in his chest and his heart was thumping despite it.

If that meant he would drown, he didn't mind. He would be drowning in her. In that scent of lemon and mint that came from he had no idea where. But it radiated off her skin, from her lips, and he'd never been a lemon and mint man until now.

His fingers stroked the skin of her arms, aware of how lucky they were to touch her. He memorised the smoothness; the bump near her right elbow where something must have bitten her; the indentations below her left shoulder where she must have got her vaccinations. She shivered when he skimmed her collarbone, when his index fingers stroked her neck. He stored the knowledge away for the future, when he could seduce her more thoroughly, when his desk and his employees weren't in the way.

That didn't stop him from giving it his best effort now.

He cupped her face, angling her into a position that would deepen their kiss. He was rewarded with her hands clinging to his waist, before they drifted up and fisted his shirt. Then they were exploring his skin, flesh to flesh somehow. He didn't know how she'd managed to slip her hands under his clothing, but he was grateful for it. Even if it did mean he'd never be able to let another person touch him this way. He couldn't; not when she was claiming him. Not when he wanted to remember her touching him. To remember how his blood seemed to follow along beneath her strokes, pulsing with need and desire, showing him what it meant to be alive. To live.

How had he not known it before?

'You're very impressive,' she said, pulling back. Her cheeks were flushed, there was a dazed half-smile on her face, and her voice was hoarse. She was the most beguiling she'd ever been. 'I don't suppose you became this way in the last few weeks?'

'I'm not sure what you mean.'

'These muscles.' She scraped her nails lightly over his skin. There was no way it would mark him, but they might as well have with the little sparks going off everywhere she touched. 'They weren't always there.'

'No,' he said slowly. 'I don't think they were when I was born. But I was an impressive toddler.' He laughed when she pinched him. 'Hey, I was using your words.'

'And being obnoxious about it.'

'I didn't want you to think I'd changed.'

Her own laugh was softer than his. Perhaps even thoughtful. 'No, I don't think you have. Even though I seem to be hoping you had. That somehow you'd become this man I'm attracted to and maybe even like in the last few weeks.' She brought her hands out from under his shirt, straightening the material as she did. 'That was what I was implying with the muscles, by the way. I know they didn't suddenly appear. I think I only just noticed them.'

Just like I only just noticed you.

She didn't have to say it. Everything she'd already said implied it. But he wanted to tell her she was wrong. He had changed. He could no longer see Lee without thinking about how Lee had used him. More importantly, what Lee had done to her. He didn't think competing with Alexa was fun any more; didn't see it as harmless. With her, he let himself be himself. He showed her that he cared for her, despite his better judgement. He let himself take care of her, was honest with her. She hadn't used those vulnerabilities against him either.

Sure, he hadn't entirely opened up to her about how he felt about his family—but then, neither had she. They were still checking one another out, tentatively testing whether they could trust the other. He thought they were there now. And he wanted to open up to her, wanted to know more about her.

'Do you want to go out with me?' he asked, desperate to do just that. 'Tonight, I mean. Do you want to go out?'

Her lips twitched; light danced in her eyes. 'Are you sure you're feeling well enough?'

'I've made a surprising recovery.'

'Must have been the same twenty-four-hour bug I had.'

'Not quite the same,' he said with a small laugh.

'Hmm. That would be slightly puzzling.'

'Only slightly.'

'Maybe you've had an elixir.'

'I have.'

He moved closer, nuzzled her neck. She angled, giving him better access.

'What are you implying?'

'You're magical.'

She laughed. Patted his chest. 'That, I know.'

'I don't doubt it.' He nipped at her lips. Then, when it felt good, kissed her again, lingering. 'Is that a yes?'

'What was the question?' she asked, voice breathy.

He chuckled. 'Can I take you somewhere?'

'I would love that.'

'I know you like kissing me—' *she hoped* '—but taking me to Lovers Lane seems like overkill.'

Benjamin laughed as he pulled into a parking space at the edge of the road. All the parking spaces on Lovers Lane were at the edge of the road. Alexa wasn't a fan of it since the road was on a cliff, which meant the edge was more dangerous than most edges. But she wasn't going to protest when Benjamin had brought her to this—admittedly—romantic place.

She also wasn't going to move.

Except to eat this broth he'd made her.

But she'd do it very, *very* slowly.

'I wanted to bring you somewhere with a nice view.'

'The quarry was nice. It didn't have such a blatant name. It was safe, too.'

'I've already taken you there.'

It was sweet enough that she leaned forward so she could see the view past his head. It looked much like the night sky itself: dark, save for the lights twinkling back at her. Those lights weren't stars, but the city of Cape Town, and they weren't demure and subtle, but brash and bright. They stretched up until the base of Table Mountain, leaving the landmark to loom over them in darkness. If the lights spoke of the city's vibrancy, its life, then the mountain anchored it. Reminded her that people had families here, careers. Generations had become stronger, less broken, more whole.

'It is pretty nice,' she said on an exhale.

He smiled.

She didn't want to be caught in it, though it was too late to be coy. She'd already given up something of herself when she'd kissed him earlier. Or had he taken it? No, she thought. The permission she'd given him meant that she'd given it willingly. It made her uncomfortable to think she had, so she was trying to blame him.

Uncomfortable didn't feel like the right word

though. It was more…like she was going into a battle for the survival of the universe and she had nothing but a sword. Perhaps not even that. Uncomfortable? Sure. Dangerous? Stupid? Completely and utterly irrational? Definitely.

She took a breath and reached into the brown bag for the broth.

'Thanks for swinging by my place to get this.'

'I could have made you a fresh batch.'

'Your kitchen was busy.' She opened the container and sighed at the aroma. 'Besides, I didn't want my first In the Rough meal to be broth.'

She closed her eyes at the first taste of it. It had been hours since she'd eaten, and because she was at the Institute, she'd settled for one slice of toast and a banana. She'd blamed it on her bug when Cherise had asked. She'd also stared longingly at the steak Cherise was eating. But there'd be plenty of steak in the future. For now, she had broth. Warm, delicious broth that wouldn't turn her stomach against her.

Was pregnancy simplifying her appetite? She hoped not.

'Technically it is your first meal from In the Rough,' he said.

'This doesn't count. It doesn't come from the restaurant.'

'Just its manager. Its once-upon-a-time head chef.'

'I forgot about that,' she said, sipping the soup.

'Did you tell me why you decided you didn't want to be head chef any more?'

'Probably not.' He paused. 'I'm happy to share. If you are.'

She frowned. 'What do you mean? I... Oh,' she said when he gestured to the brown bag that still had his food in it. 'Sorry. I got distracted.'

'Yes, I got that.' He was smiling when she handed him his food. He went to open it, but stopped himself. Opened a window instead. Looked at her. 'The smell probably wouldn't be good if you're nauseous.'

'No,' she murmured, touched. 'Thank you.'

'No problem.'

He opened her window, too, and only then dug into his food. It was lasagne, and her mind salivated over it if not her stomach. She'd steered away from rich food the last three months, with good reason, but she missed the taste of pasta and red meat and bacon. Sighing a little, she took another spoonful of broth.

'I wanted a change,' he said between bites. 'And I thought I was capable of more than being in a kitchen. The idea of running the restaurant intrigued me.'

'Did it live up to your expectations?'

'It did.' His mouth lifted on one side. 'I think I lived up to its expectations, too.'

'If that's your way of giving yourself a compliment, you didn't have to. I could have told you that you were doing a good job.'

'But would you have?'

'Maybe. After some coercing.'

'Of what kind?' His voice had dropped seductively. He leaned closer, but she pulled back. 'What's wrong?'

'I can't kiss you when you're eating that.'

'Oh.' He frowned down at the food, as if it had betrayed him. As if he couldn't believe that it had. 'I wasn't thinking.'

'You were, but not with...' She broke off with a demure smile. 'I'm not going to be crass.' She patted his cheek. 'But yes, that would have been appropriate coercion.'

'Seems a little cruel to remind me when I can't do it.'

'I can be a little cruel sometimes.'

With a small smile that seemed to say *I know*— which pleased her more than offended her—he asked, 'Why did you stop being head chef?'

'I never was. Well,' she reconsidered, 'a lot of my responsibilities blurred the lines with the position, but I knew that I wanted to have other input than in the kitchen to make Infinity the best it could be. I also wanted the business to run independently of me. Or I guess I wanted to run independently of the business.'

'So you could have a life.'

'And maybe babies.'

'You thought about babies then?'

'I suppose I did, though it wasn't "oh, I should do this to have babies".' She set the spoon against the rim of the container. 'I knew I didn't want my life to look like my parents'. Mostly business,' she clarified when she realised he wouldn't know. 'They work a lot, enjoy it, barely spend time at home. I wanted to have more than that. I wanted to have a family. I forgot about it while I tried to get Infinity up and running. Then after an employee brought her kid to work, it hit me: I wanted a home life, too. With babies.'

'That's why your place is so homey.'

'You still sound surprised.'

'Not surprised—jealous. I would love to be so intentional about…everything.' He closed the container his food was in. 'I spent a lot of my time not doing what I wanted to do. When I got to do it, I realised it wasn't really what I wanted to do.'

'But you're there now, aren't you?' she asked. 'You like running the restaurant.'

'Yeah.'

'Great. So you got there in your professional life. Just figure out how to get there in your personal life.'

'Easier said than done.'

'Of course. But you're the only one who can do it.' She closed the container her own food was in and put it in the brown bag. Did the same for his when he handed it to her. 'You can live your life doing the easy thing and going with the flow. It'll take you where you need to be, but maybe there'll be more pit stops. Maybe it'll make you feel as if you should have done more. But—' she dragged the word out '—taking the harder route and doing things intentionally will help you feel proud. Things might still take a long time, but you'll appreciate the journey more.'

She shook her head, rolled her eyes. 'I know I sound silly.'

'You don't. It's…harder, with my mom.'

'How?'

'She needs me,' he said simply. 'If I'm not around, she'll push too hard. My father would be alone to help her with it. It's how our family is.'

'Would you move out if she didn't need you?'

'I… Yeah, maybe.' His lips pursed, then parted to let an exhale through. 'Probably. I'm over thirty,' he said with a quick laugh. 'I shouldn't be living with my parents any more.'

'That's why you're taking me to Lovers Lane instead of home. Not that you should take me home.' She closed her eyes. 'I didn't mean it that way.'

'I know. But maybe that's what you get for being a little cruel.'

He laughed when she punched him lightly in the shoulder. They sat in companionable silence until he said, 'It's cool. The way you've crafted your life. Not everyone can do that.'

She leaned back against the seat. 'I have my parents to thank for that, I guess. For all their faults, they were very clear about having a plan. It was a set plan for them—school, university, work—and they weren't thrilled that mine looked a little different. But I did have one. They just didn't see it.'

She'd faltered at the end, so she shouldn't have been surprised at the hand Benjamin reached out and took hers with. Not even the way he lifted her hand to kiss it should have surprised her. Maybe it was the warmth that spread through her body because of his actions that did. The way it settled in her chest, soothing the holes in her heart her parents had created with their rigidity.

'I'm sure they're proud of you.'

'Maybe.' She reclined the seat with her free hand. Settled both their hands on her stomach. 'I guess they are now. Though they would most likely prefer me to be a business mogul like Lee is. One successful business pales in comparison to that.'

'Which is what he intended,' Benjamin said softly. When she lifted her gaze to him, the edge of his mouth lifted. 'You've told me a lot. I can piece together the rest.'

'So it seems.' She ran the index finger of the hand that wasn't tangled with his over his skin. 'Lee's ambitious. Smart. I like to think those things were the primary motivations.'

'But you know they're not.'

She couldn't admit it out loud, so she hedged. 'Our parents taught us to be the best. I took that to mean people outside of our family. Lee took it to mean…me.' She swallowed. 'But it gave us both motivation, thinking that. If I'm part of it, it's only because of that.'

He tugged at her hand. Frowning, she looked at him. His face was serious, but other than that, she couldn't read his emotion.

'What?' she asked.

'Why are you protecting him?'

'I'm not…' She broke off at his look. 'I'm his sister. His older sister. That's what I'm supposed to do.'

'By that logic, he should be looking up to you, his older sister. Not competing with you so much you've lost your ability to trust people who care about you.'

The shock had her pulling her hand out of his, grabbing a hold of her stomach with both hands. She wasn't sure whether she thought she was protecting herself, or her children. Didn't know why she thought she had to do either.

'Lex—'

'No, give me a moment.' Purposefully, she leaned back against the chair, relaxed her body. She smoothed her clothing, took a couple of deep breaths, let her mind settle. When she was ready, or as ready as she would ever be, she nodded.

'You're right. I realise this. Which is why I've chosen not to have him in my life.'

'I'm sorry. I shouldn't have said that.'

'Stop apologising, Ben,' she said softly. 'You keep doing it.'

'Because I keep messing up.'

'Being honest, caring… That's not messing up.' She bit the inside of her lip at his expression. Tried to fix it. 'Don't get me wrong, it's very inconvenient. Especially when you're trying to avoid your issues. Don't you dare apologise!' she said when he opened his mouth.

He gave her a wry grin and she laughed.

'It's like a disease with you.'

'I can't help it.'

'Sure you can. Just stop doing it.'

'I've been doing it my entire life.'

'Why?'

He didn't reply immediately, his expression contorted in confusion. 'I don't actually know.' He tried to hide the panic that answer brought by giving her a smile. She wondered if he knew how horribly he was failing.

'Okay, we're going to play a game.'

'A game?'

'It's a distraction, Foster.'

'In that case, tell me,' Benjamin said with a smile. It was more genuine now.

'Well, I'm going to try to get you to apologise to me, and you're going to resist.'

'What are you going to do?'

'Nothing specific,' she replied nonchalantly. 'You know that game where, when you're on a road trip, you pick a colour and have to count the number of cars in that colour?'

'Yeah...'

'That's how it's going to be. When the opportunity arises.' She brought a finger under her nose, pretending to stifle a sneeze. 'Oh, my sinuses are acting up.'

'Should I close the windows?'

'Just a little.' She pretended to stop another sneeze. 'Do you have tissues or something here?'

'Yeah, I do,' he said, just as she knew he would.

He reached for the pack of tissues in his door, reached out to give it to her. She held out a hand, but moved it slightly when he tried to drop the tissues into it. The pack fell between the seats.

'Oh. Sorry about that. I thought...' He broke off when he saw her shaking her head. When he saw the smile on her face, too. 'You planned that?'

'Yes. And you failed. Terribly. In the first minute of the game.'

'But that wasn't fair!'

'All's fair in love and war.' When there was an awkward silence, she wrinkled her nose. 'This is war, in case you were wondering.'

'I wasn't.'

But, if she was being honest with herself, she was.

CHAPTER SIXTEEN

WHAT WAS THE SAYING? *Going to hell in a handbasket?* If so, that was exactly what was happening. The handbasket was filled with delicious food courtesy of Cherise, but the tying of the bow, the giving? That was all Lee.

'You invited your sister?' Benjamin hissed the moment he saw Alexa walk into the hotel ballroom.

Okay, not the moment he saw Alexa. The moment he saw Alexa he stopped, his brain stopped, and he was pretty sure his heart stopped. She looked…amazing. It was too inadequate a word, but he clung to it. The gown she wore was somewhere between coral and peach, the colour of it magnificent against the bronze of her skin. It was a halter-neck dress that clung to her chest, ending just below her breasts in a cinch, before flowing down over the rest of her. The material was pleated, and when she moved, it moved with her. When she was still, those pleats created the illusion of space. All for the benefit of hiding the bump he knew was growing by the day.

The reason he knew it was because he'd found a reason, every day since they'd been to Lovers Lane, to see her. He didn't once go to her restaurant—he worried that would be invading her personal space—but he visited her flat under the guise of bringing more food. He asked her to go out for tea under the pretence of picking her brains about something. It had been a week and a half of this, where he was clearly making up reasons to see her, but she never once called him out on it.

He told himself that if she'd wanted to, she would have. She wasn't the kind of person not to. The fact that she wasn't saying anything told him she wanted to see him, too. As did the small, private smile she smiled every time she saw him.

The days she invited him in were the ones he liked best. Her flat was fast becoming his favourite place, in no small part because they could be whoever they wanted to be there. Turned out, they wanted to be friends. The kissing that happened quite frequently—and sometimes progressed to other things, but never far enough to undermine their friendship—was merely a bonus. But things were so easy between them when they were there. He told her about how he'd grown up trying to help his parents; she told him how she'd grown up trying to make hers proud. They comforted one another, teased one another, and, yes, kissed and touched, and it was all magnificent.

And it was going to end.

'I didn't invite her,' Lee said slowly. 'She wouldn't have come if she'd known the invitation was from me.'

Benjamin resisted grabbing the man at the front of his collar. 'What did you do?' he said through his teeth.

'Used the grapevine.' Lee smirked. 'It still works.'

It took Benjamin a long time to remember what he was like when he wasn't so damn angry. Not that anger was such a bad thing. It gave him a clarity he hadn't had before. Sure, some of that clarity was also because of his conversations with Alexa, but it was clarity nevertheless. And he knew exactly what he had to do.

'I quit.'

'What?'

'Resign, effective immediately.'

'You can't do that,' Lee spluttered. 'Your contract says you have to give me at least a month's notice.'

'Then you have it.'

'What the hell?' Lee's expression was stormy. 'This is because of my sister, isn't it? She poached you.' He shook his head in disbelief. 'You let her? You let her because you're sleeping with her?'

'Lee,' he warned.

Lee took a breath, clearly trying to get hold of his emotions. 'You can't do this, man. We've been working together for years. I gave you a chance. You can't walk out on me.'

'I'm grateful for what you did for me.' And he meant it. But the weight that had lifted from his shoulders the moment he'd quit told him he'd needed to. 'Truly, I am. You're an incredible businessman. I've learnt a lot from you. I have no doubt I could have learnt more.'

'Then why are you leaving?'

'Because you used me to beat your sister.' Saying it out loud made Benjamin feel in control. As if finally, after all those people had used him, he'd regained what they'd taken from him. His pride, perhaps. Or perhaps it was that he was no longer scared of saying it. 'And you're malicious. To your own sister, who's done nothing but love you.'

'Is that what she told you?' Lee scoffed. 'She must be really good in…'

He broke off when Benjamin, quick as lightning, took his arm. 'I'm warning you about what you say next.'

Lee's chest heaved. 'Okay. I'm sorry.'

He let go. 'I appreciate that.'

'You're serious about this?'

'Deadly.' He straightened his tie. 'I respect who you are in business, but not as a man. I can't, knowing how you've treated the woman I… I love.'

He'd hesitated in speech, just as he had with his feelings. But he could see they'd been there long before the last month. The moment he'd seen her in that class, he'd tumbled. Knocked his head in the process, it seemed, because he went back to being a kid and tried to compete with her so she would notice him.

But she'd never allowed him close enough to see that she had noticed him; not in the way he'd intended. He'd reminded her of her brother, the man, he suspected, had hurt her most. She seemed to have some kind of resignation about who her parents were, but not with Lee. With Lee, she'd tried, and he'd brushed her away. When she let Benjamin in the last few weeks, he could see how much it hurt her—and how much he had hurt her, simply by acting like a teenage fool.

Now what he had seen, what she'd allowed him to see, convinced him that if he hadn't been a fool, he would have had these feelings aeons ago. She might not have iced him out, and he might have seen who she really was. That was who he was in love with. The woman who wasn't even a little cruel. Who was passionate and driven and who cared about people.

It was the biggest honour of his life that she'd chosen to open up to him. She'd let him see her vulnerable, and he hoped with all his might he'd done enough to show her she could be vulnerable with him. He knew she struggled with it, and if he had to be patient he would be, simply because she was worth it.

If he had to spend his entire lifetime proving that she could trust him, he would. Because he loved her. And she deserved it.

He had to tell her.

'Benjamin!'

The exclamation came from a short distance away. When he turned towards it, he saw Cherise.

'Thanks so much for coming,' she said, stopping in front of him. 'I thought I should show you what I can do, too, since I hope we can work together.'

It was what he'd wanted to hear most, once upon a time. Now, what he wanted to hear most was Alexa's voice, saying anything, really, but mostly talking about them sharing a future together. He turned, barely thinking about the fact that Cherise was there, waiting for an answer.

He didn't think about it at all when he saw Lee follow Alexa out of the ballroom.

The moment she saw him walking towards her she knew.

It was silly of her to think that she could walk into an event being catered by Cherise to get another opportunity to speak with her. To perhaps even see her in action. Alexa had found out about the charity event through an acquaintance, thought it would be harmless and beneficial, considering she hadn't heard from Cherise for over a week. When she saw Lee, it all fell into place: she hadn't heard from Cherise for a reason, she'd been set up, and she shouldn't have come.

She didn't give the gorgeous ballroom and its glistening lights and formal guests any more thought. She walked out, down the brick steps, past the fountain. She was on the small stretch of grass between the fountain and the car park when Lee caught up with her.

'Leaving so soon?'

She stopped. Closed her eyes. Turned to face him. 'Sorry I didn't stay for the *gotcha*. That's what you wanted to say, isn't it?'

'No one forced you to be here,' Lee said calmly. 'Although I'm surprised you didn't accompany Ben.' He pretended to think about it. 'Is it that he didn't tell you about this, or that you really are trying to keep your personal and professional lives separate?'

He hadn't told her, though she didn't need to tell Lee that. Nor did she have to figure out why Benjamin hadn't said anything. He was protecting her, or maybe himself, and though she understood it—he was so used to protecting the people in his life—it bothered her on a deep level. But that wasn't important now.

'Look, Lee, I don't want to stick around for the gloating, okay?'

'Not even your own?'

'What are you talking about?'

'Oh, you're going to pretend you didn't ask him to do it. That seems like an odd position, all things considered.'

'Tell me, or let me go,' she said sharply.

'Your boyfriend quit.'

'He what?'

His brows rose. 'Nice acting, Sis. Didn't know you had it in you.'

'He quit? Why?' She narrowed her eyes. 'What the hell did you do?'

'Absolutely nothing.' Though she could barely see it, she knew he was biting the inside of his lip. He used to do it when they were younger, on the side. 'He told me it's because of the way I've been treating you.'

She caught the swear word before it left her lips. Mentally, though, she let the curses fly. The idiot! It was fine if he kept things from her because he thought he was protecting her—okay, not fine, understandable—but this? This was stupid. This was his entire future. It was his life. And he was doing it for her! It seemed much too much for people who'd been close for less than two weeks. This felt more like a gesture; something someone did before proclaiming their love or something.

A thin thread of panic wove between the synapses in her brain. It threatened to overcome her, and for a second she thought she would fall over. But that would hurt her babies, and she had to be strong. She couldn't let them suffer for things she was responsible for.

She looked at her brother. Realised she needed to sort this out if she wanted to keep that promise to her kids.

'If I talk to him, convince him to go back to

you, would you leave me alone?' She could already see, before he even said it, that he was going to make some stupid remark. 'I'm being serious. If I get Ben to go back to In the Rough, I don't want to see or hear from you again. Unless there's a family function, which, fortunately, doesn't happen often. But outside of that. No surprises. No manipulation. Nothing.'

'You really want that?'

He'd taken the stance of a victim, his voice hurt and surprised, as if he had no contribution to why she wanted this. It made her snap.

'What I want is to have a brother who doesn't make me feel as if I have to walk carefully everywhere I go in case he pulls the rug out from under me. I want to have a brother who doesn't *enjoy* pulling the rug out from under me. Who, when I fall, asks me why I'm on the ground. Who gets upset when I refuse his help.'

She'd never spent enough time with Lee to learn how his expressions revealed his emotions. Or maybe it was that the only expressions he wore around her were variations of smugness or satisfaction or a combination of the two. So she couldn't tell how he felt now, because none of that came through in his expression.

'I thought… This is what we do, Lex. We compete with one another. We make one another better.'

'What? That's what you think this is? No—*how*

do you think that is what this is?' Her voice was high with disbelief. She didn't try to temper it. 'You competed with me, Lee. I *congratulated* you for beating my records, or scoring higher than me.'

'You were conceding.'

'Conceding…'

Now she recognised the look on Lee's face: bewilderment. He genuinely didn't understand why she was so upset. She nearly laughed. He was the least self-aware person she knew.

'I wasn't conceding. I was sincerely wishing you well because I was happy for you. At first. I could see competing with me made you happy and gave you purpose and I wanted you to have that.' She took a steadying breath. 'But you didn't want me to be happy. If you did, you would have supported me the way I supported you. You would have taken the hand I held out every time I asked you to go to a movie with me, or watch a show, or do whatever stupid things brothers and sisters do together. But you said no. Instead you tried to beat me at things that didn't even matter.'

She folded her arms, suddenly cold.

'And you tried to beat me at things that did matter, too.' She blinked when that made her want to cry. 'You bought the building I spent months trying to find. Months,' she said with a shake of her head. 'I did research into who I was buying the building from, into the neighbourhood, into how much it would cost to renovate, how long it would take. Then you swooped in and stole it. Just stole it.' She lifted a hand, dropped it. 'The only thing you knew about it was that I wanted it.'

'I... I didn't realise.'

'You didn't realise that you'd destroyed my dream?' she asked. 'Of both that restaurant and ever having a normal relationship with you?'

He didn't reply, though he ran his hand over his hair a few times, lips moving without sound. He looked at her, and if she wasn't so numb by the conversation, she would have been touched by the vulnerability she saw there.

But she was numb. She had to be. If she wasn't, the reminder of all the times she'd wanted to forge a relationship with her brother would have consumed her. The hope she'd once had was enmeshed in those memories. She'd desperately wanted to shield herself against her parents, had known that if Lee was behind the shield with her she could be stronger. *They* would be stronger together. Except Lee chose to wield their parents' weapons against her, too, even when she'd surrendered.

She wasn't surrendering any more. It might have seemed as if she was by offering Lee Benjamin, but she knew she wasn't. She was lifting her shield, protecting herself once more. Because the only way she could truly do that against her brother was by coming to a truce with him. Which meant he needed to make the decision, too.

She could smell the faint smoke of guilt at using

Benjamin as a pawn, but maybe he would understand. He might even be grateful that he wouldn't have to protect her any more.

'You don't, um…' Lee cleared his throat. 'You don't have to get Benjamin to work for me.'

She just studied him.

'I'll leave you alone. I didn't realise…' Now he shook his head. 'I'll leave you alone. I promise.'

She almost ran a hand over her stomach before she remembered Lee didn't know about her pregnancy. She settled for clasping her hands over the bag she'd brought with her.

'Thank you.'

Neither of them moved. But there was a movement behind Lee. Alexa's eyes automatically shifted to it, before she realised it was Benjamin. Her body wanted to sag against something, let it hold up her weight as she prepared for another conversation that would leave her raw. It was so different to how her body had responded to Benjamin in the last weeks. With relief, excitement, attraction, desire. She'd felt safer than at any other time in her life.

This interaction with Lee seemed to prove how much safety was an illusion.

CHAPTER SEVENTEEN

'ARE YOU OKAY?'

It was the first thing that came into his mind when he reached her, but he immediately realised it was a stupid question. Of course she wasn't okay. He could see it in her stance, in her eyes, in the brittle tone of her voice when she lied and told him she was. She looked broken, tired, and he hated the person who'd put that look on her face.

He turned to Lee. 'Leave.'

Lee looked at Alexa, then back at him. Uncharacteristically withdrawn, he nodded. After one last glance at Alexa, a parting of the lips that made it seem as though he wanted to say something, he turned around and walked away. Benjamin waited until he was out of sight, then turned.

'Come on, let's find somewhere to sit down.'

She didn't fight him on it, and his worry kicked up another notch. But he kept it inside long enough to find a bench. The restaurant was in a vineyard, much like most prestigious restaurants in Cape Town. But instead of looking out onto the vineyard, the restaurant looked out over the stretch of property on the opposite side of it. It was mostly grass and a long deck that went out into a pond. The pond was still, though Benjamin saw the occasional disturbance of water and the rings that resulted from that disturbance. He watched it for a long time, waiting for Alexa to recover from whatever had happened with Lee.

When he thought she might have, he asked, 'Did that go okay?'

'He agreed to leave me alone, so I guess so.'

'That's what you wanted?'

'I asked for it.'

But she didn't say it was what she wanted, and he had a feeling it wasn't. He wasn't sure if she knew that though, or if she needed to figure it out. He wasn't sure about his position in this either: Should he prod? Give her space? Point her in the right direction? None of the options seemed right. He didn't speak, crippled by the indecision.

'Did you quit your job?' she said into the silence.

'He told you?'

'Accused me,' she corrected. 'Apparently I've been using you to get to him.'

'Sounds diabolical.'

'You can't say I didn't warn you.' She opened her palms on her lap, looking at them, not him. He should have taken it as sign, prepared himself. Because he didn't, he was completely taken aback by her next words. 'I hope you didn't do this because of me.'

'No. Of course not.'

'You didn't quit because of me?'

'No.'

'Then why did you?'

'I…couldn't work with him any more. He got you here because he wanted to…' He broke off at her look. 'Fine, maybe it had something to do with you. But it wasn't *because* of you.'

She threaded her fingers together. 'You're going to regret it.' Her voice was neutral. 'You're going to blame me when you regret it.'

'I won't.'

'You will. Unless you can tell me you're leaving because of more than just me.'

'I…want to do my own thing.'

'Liar.'

'I'm not lying,' he snapped. Took a breath. 'I shouldn't have said that. It was—' he relaxed his jaw '—uncalled for.'

'It was, especially since it's the truth.'

'It's not fair,' he replied, barely retaining control over his anger. 'It was never fair of you to expect me to work with a man I don't respect any more.'

'You shouldn't have let the way he treated me affect your working relationship.'

'He used me to get to you.' He stood now. Walked away, trying to keep that control. Came back when it didn't help him have more of it. 'Do you know how many people have used me in my life? Too many,' he answered for her. 'It was worse that he did it to get to you. It was worse that he was still so terrible to you. How can you ask me to ignore it?'

'Because of this!' she exclaimed, shifting to the edge of the bench. 'You quit your job. The one you love, at the restaurant you built. Don't you see that? Don't you see you're going to lose everything you've worked for all because of me?' She dropped her head. 'One day you'll think I used you for this, too. I almost did.' Her voice was barely above a whisper. 'I told him that if I got you to work for him again, he had to leave me alone.'

He took the time he needed to work through that.

'Because you care,' he said, crouching down so he could see her face. 'You know what the restaurant means to me.'

'Maybe. Maybe I did it because it meant getting what I want.'

Her eyes, defiant, met his.

'You're saying this to hurt me,' he said, realising it. 'You're pushing me away.'

'Yes,' she whispered. 'You deserve more than me. You deserve someone who can care as much as you do. Selflessly. I… I can't.'

He froze. Slowly, he rose. He rubbed a hand over his face. 'Why not?'

'Can't you see?' She was sitting up, spine

straight. It looked so out of place against the curved back of the bench. 'You're selfless. You protect the people you care about at all costs. Even if you're lying to them.'

He could hardly deny it when that was exactly what he'd done that day.

'I've been alone most of my life. I'm used to thinking about myself. More importantly—' she took a deep breath '—I can't trust someone who won't tell me the truth. And I can't keep worrying that I'm keeping you from doing what you want to do. But if I don't, you'll keep putting yourself last.'

'It's not... I'm not...' He exhaled. 'Why don't we talk about you being unable to accept when people try to care for you?'

She bit her lip. 'Okay. What about it would you like to discuss?'

It took him a moment to get over his surprise. 'Why?'

'Why can't I accept people caring for me?' she asked. He nodded. A short moment later, she continued. 'Because it goes away. In some shape or form, I'll discover I can't trust them. It goes away, Ben.' There was a quick inhale of air. When he moved to her, she held out a hand to stop him. Sniffed. 'No, I'm okay.' But two tears streamed down each of her cheeks. She wiped at them quickly. 'I don't want to go through that.'

'It doesn't just go away.' He went to sit next to her, as far away as the bench allowed so she had her space. 'I can't care one day and stop caring the other.'

'But you can *think* you care one day and realise you don't the other.'

'Has this happened to you?'

'No. I wouldn't let it.'

'You mean you haven't let anyone close enough to allow it to happen.'

She inclined her head in acknowledgement.

'That's not healthy.'

'It's safe.'

'Safe isn't going to give you happiness.'

'Are you speaking from experience?' she asked blandly. 'You're staying at home so you can be safe, so you can protect your mother and help your father. So you don't have to face your real feelings about your family.'

He stared at her. 'There are no feelings.'

'So you're happy?' she prodded. 'You're safe and happy, the ultimate juxtaposition, according to you?'

He stood again. 'This isn't fair.'

'It is, but you don't like it.' She stood now, too. 'Which is fine. You don't have to like it.'

'You're using this as an excuse to push me away.'

'I don't need an excuse. I've told you every reason we can't continue this.' She gestured between them.

'You're really that scared of trusting someone?' he asked. 'Is being alone better than taking a chance?'

She folded her arms, the line of her mouth flat. 'Yes. I've spent my life learning that lesson. I won't let anyone hurt me the way my family has.'

'Even if it means pushing away someone who—' he swallowed. Said it anyway. Because he was a fool '—loves you?'

She blinked. Again, and again, until her lashes were fluttering like the wings of a butterfly. He tried to give her a moment to process. He couldn't.

'I haven't once let you down, Alexa. I've been there for you since this entire thing with Lee started. I lied, yes, but I thought...' He shook his head. 'I wasn't doing it to hurt you. The very opposite, in fact.' He took a step closer. 'Trust me. Trust me because I love you, and I'll try to do better because I love you. Trust me because I've shown you that you can.'

She was shaking her head before he had finished speaking. 'You need to care about yourself, too, in order to love, Ben. I don't think you do.'

With that, she walked away.

It had not been a good week. Someone had forgotten to order the seafood for the restaurant on Monday. It meant that Alexa had to remove all relevant dishes from the menu, make thousands of apologies, and offer substitutes. Then, on Wednesday, someone had forgotten about the staff meeting, come in late, and the event that was being hosted that evening had a few hiccups because the meeting hadn't proceeded.

Everyone made mistakes. She tried to remember that on Friday evening, when she was dead on her feet and contemplating disciplinary action. It complicated things that she'd been the someone who'd forgotten and needed to be punished. Maybe she would get her staff to give her a roasting. Making fun of her would hopefully rebuild the morale that seemed to be lacking, too.

'Hey.' Kenya appeared in her doorway, leaning against the frame of it as though she'd always been there. She was holding two bottles of beer. 'I thought you could use one?'

'Thanks, but I can't drink it.'

Kenya's brow quirked. 'Since when are you this strict about alcohol on a Friday night?'

She couldn't be bothered to keep it a secret any more. She was almost sixteen weeks pregnant with twins, her body was becoming fuller by the day, her plan to have the restaurant secured before her maternity leave had imploded, and she was tired of keeping it all to herself. At least before, she'd had Benjamin to confide in. That was no longer an option. She tried not to listen to the crack of her heart at that thought.

'Since I got pregnant.'

'You're pregnant?' Kenya stepped inside the office, slammed the door, and then put both beers on Alexa's desk. 'Who do I have to kill?'

'Why are you killing someone?' Alexa asked with a laugh.

'Because they knocked you up! Unless...' She eyed Alexa suspiciously 'Did you want to be knocked up?'

'Yes.'

'Oh.' Kenya frowned. 'You trapped them.'

She chuckled again. 'I didn't trap anyone. I went to a sperm bank because your family made me remember how much I wanted my own. How soon I wanted it, too.' She shrugged and let out a small smile. 'Anyway, that's why I've been dressing like this. Trying to hide the bump.'

'I was wondering.' Kenya dropped into the chair on the visitor's side of Alexa's desk. She drank her beer. 'Honestly, I thought you were going through a boho chic period.'

'Seriously?'

'I didn't want to limit you with my expectations of who you are.' Kenya smiled, but it lacked its fire. Alexa found out why a couple of seconds later. 'Why didn't you tell me you were doing this? I could have come with you. Supported you. From what I know about the process, it isn't easy.'

'No, it isn't. And honestly? I could have used the support.' Her heart ached at the acknowledgement. 'But I'm an idiot.' She offered Kenya a small smile. 'I thought that if I let you in, you'd hurt me. I've got so used to doing things on my own, I thought I could do this.'

She wasn't talking about conceiving her children any more, and they both knew it.

'Why would you think that?' Kenya's voice was soft, and a little judgemental. Alexa smiled.

'It's what I'm used to,' she said. 'My family is messed up. And every time I thought something was going right, it was really...not.'

She should have explained it better, but it occurred to her that she hadn't told Kenya anything of her personal life. She knew that Kenya had three older brothers, seven nieces, one nephew and a daughter, and that motherhood had pushed her to finally get the therapy she thought she needed. Alexa knew all of that, but she hadn't told Kenya one thing about her family.

'It's a long story, and I should have told you more of it sooner,' she said softly.

Kenya didn't blink. 'You should have, yes.'

'I'm sorry. For all of it.'

'Good.' Kenya didn't look away as she drank from her beer. 'So, should we thank the pregnancy for this stupendous week, or the family?'

'Neither. Or maybe the family? I don't know.' It was the perfect opportunity to make things right with Kenya. Or at least to start to. 'I think it's mostly because of the fake boyfriend.'

'Explain.'

So she did. She told Kenya about her terrible

brother, who'd inspired her to pretend her rival was her boyfriend. How Benjamin had gone along with it, even after he'd found out she was pregnant. She told Kenya about the twins—to which she got a colourful reply—and about how things had snowballed, but in a nice way, with Benjamin. And then how it had all melted, leaving her feeling as though she was drowning.

She ended on an apology, because she'd been a bad friend and a worse boss. She couldn't secure the restaurant before she was on maternity leave. She could probably still try, but time was running out and—

'Firstly,' Kenya interrupted, 'you've been a pretty terrible friend. There's no way you're worse as a boss.'

'Wow. Thanks.'

'Secondly,' Kenya continued with a grin, 'we haven't had a head chef for almost four months now. I know you've been picking up a lot of the slack, but that's because you didn't trust us—' she gave Alexa a look '—to help you with it. You don't have to kill yourself to find a replacement chef before you go on leave. If you do, great, and we'll help train them. If you don't, we'll survive.'

Kenya leaned forward and rested a hand on Alexa's.

'Babe, you've built a damn good team. You've also earned our loyalty. That includes helping out when things get rough.' She squeezed. 'It includes taking care of things while you have your babies. We could probably help you get ready for the babies, too.'

'Oh, that's not—' She cut herself off. 'Thank you,' she said instead. 'That means a lot.'

'Yeah, well, it should.' Kenya softened her words with a smile. 'You mean a lot to us.'

'And you mean a lot to me.'

Kenya blinked. Then took the last swig of her beer. 'Thanks. Now, let's go tell the people out there you're having two babies.'

'Oh. Oh, yeah. Okay.'

'It's been a rough week for all of us. This would help. But only if you want to do it.'

She thought about it for a long time. Then she nodded and stood up. 'Let's go.'

The reaction was more than she could have ever anticipated or expected. A stunned silence followed her words, but after that someone began to cheer. People came forward to congratulate her, offering her words of encouragement and advice, asking how they could help.

Alexa swallowed down her emotion many times in the next hour, her eyes prickling at the support she had no idea she'd already had. When she caught Kenya's eye later, she got a wink and a knowing look in return. It made the tears she was holding back run down her cheeks, and she was immediately handed tissues from three different directions. She laughed, waved off concern, pressed the tissue to her eyes. And in that moment she realised two things:

One, she'd spent so many years afraid of opening up and trusting people. Yet despite that, she'd found the very family she'd hoped for her entire life. And they trusted her, for whatever reason. Apparently, she'd earned it. Maybe it was time that she allowed herself to see they'd earned her trust, too.

Number two was more complicated. Because the entire time she'd experienced this emotional, overwhelming thing, she'd felt as though she were missing a limb. She didn't let herself think of it until she was alone that night in her flat. When she did, she didn't like that Benjamin had wedged himself so deeply in her mind that she couldn't go through her day without thinking about him. That she couldn't have important experiences without wanting him there. Without having him there.

She settled on the sofa, but it smelled like him, so she moved. It didn't make sense—he hadn't been there in over a week and her sofas were regularly cleaned.

Except it *did* make sense. She just didn't want to face it.

At some point during the night as she tossed and turned, she realised she already had. She knew exactly what the problem was: Benjamin hadn't wedged himself in her mind; he'd wedged himself into her heart.

pressed the tissue to her eyes. And in that moment
she realised two things . . .

One, she'd spent so many years afraid of opening up and trusting people. Yet despite that, she'd
found the very family she'd hoped for her entire
life. And they loved her, seemingly for no reason.
Apparently she'd earned it. Maybe it was time
that she allowed herself to see that she'd earned her
trust, too.

CHAPTER EIGHTEEN

HE'D NEVER THOUGHT his dream job would become
a nightmare. But it was. Working in a place he
loved but had given up for—his darkest moments
in the last week had made him think—nothing.
He only had himself to blame. Alexa hadn't asked
him to do this, neither had Lee. He'd done it because he'd thought he was being principled.

He *was* being principled. He couldn't work for
a man like Lee. Someone whose cruelty would
one day be turned on Benjamin or their staff.
Benjamin would have left then anyway, so he'd
just hurried along the inevitable by handing in
his notice.

But principles didn't pay the bills, or help the
mind when dreams were dashed. The euphoria
he'd felt after saying he was leaving was well and
truly gone. Now he only thought of his responsibilities, of what his parents would say when he
finally told them what he'd done, and how Alexa
had walked away from his proclamation of love.

A knock brought him out of his thoughts.

It was Saturday night after the restaurant had already closed and most of his staff had gone home. Lee's appearance in his doorway was perplexing for more than that reason though. The very fact that he was there after a week of radio silence was troubling. So was the fact that he'd knocked, which he never had, in all the years they'd worked together, done.

'Can I come in?'

Benjamin opened a hand, gesturing to the chair opposite him. He tried not to think about how Alexa had filled it almost three weeks before. Or anything else they'd done in the office.

'I'm surprised to see you here,' Benjamin said.

'I should have come earlier.'

'Should you have?'

Lee smiled at the casual comment. Or maybe not smiled, but Benjamin didn't think there was a description for Lee simply showing his teeth.

'Yes. We should have had a meeting to discuss the implications of your resignation and the transition plans. Have you told the staff yet?'

'No.'

'Great. We'll—'

'Lee,' Benjamin interjected. 'Did you really come here this time on a Saturday night to talk business?'

'No,' he said after a moment. He leaned forward, rested his arms on his knees. 'I'm here to apologise.'

'Apologise?'

'For setting this in motion.' Now he clasped his hands. 'I always knew you were ambitious, and that In the Rough wasn't where you'd end up. But… I sped it up, by acting like a complete jerk to Alexa. And to you. I'm sorry.'

Benjamin sat back and let his mind figure out what was happening and what he should say next. 'I appreciate that. I'm more concerned about whether you're extending that apology to Alexa.'

'No.' Lee looked down. 'She doesn't want to see me. I want to respect that.'

'I bet she'd want to see you if you're intending on apologising.'

'You think?'

'You spent your life torturing her. I think an apology would be a nice change of pace.'

Lee winced, but he straightened and ran a hand over his face. 'I don't know how I didn't see how much I was hurting her.'

'We all have blind spots when it comes to family.'

It was one of the little nuggets of wisdom his brain had come up with at three or so in the morning some time in the past week.

'Yeah, but hurting her?' He shook his head. 'That's more than a blind spot. It's…' His voice faded, and for a while after, he didn't speak. 'It's not what a brother should do to his sister.'

'Agreed.'

Lee nodded. Got up. 'I don't have anything else to say right now.'

'You could talk about the transition.'

He laughed a little. 'That was me hedging so I wouldn't have to apologise.'

Benjamin chuckled, too. 'I've been there.'

Lee walked to the door but, before he left, turned back. 'We do have to talk about the transition.'

'I know.'

'Maybe we could talk about you buying this place from me.'

'What?'

'It's lost its appeal, now that I know what it did to Alexa.' He angled his head. 'This seems like a good way to restore balance.'

'You should sell it to her, then.'

'Are you kidding me? Her place is much more popular than this. It would be a downgrade.'

With a quick wink, Lee was gone.

He hadn't left things any worse than the way he'd found them. Not even his offer to sell the place to Benjamin had made much of an impact. Perhaps because Benjamin already knew the answer: he wanted In the Rough. He wanted to run the business himself, and do things the way he'd learnt to do them. He had no doubt he would make mistakes, but that was part of the package. He was very much looking forward to making mistakes, in fact.

So yeah, he'd been lying to himself when he said he didn't know why he'd decided to leave. He'd done that because he wanted something else. But he'd also done it because he was standing up to Lee—because he was standing up for Alexa. It smarted that she didn't want him to do that. It hurt that he'd offered and she'd rejected him. She couldn't see that he wanted to do this, that he needed to, so that he could make up for…

He paused. He didn't have to make up for anything. He'd already apologised to Alexa for what he'd done to her before he'd known her. He'd tried his best to show her none of that would happen again. Why had his brain automatically gone there, then? To make up for something, as if he were in the wrong?

Because he'd taken responsibility for her life in some ways, he realised. He thought he could make the hurt she'd been through better by protecting her. But she was right: the way he'd protected her was all wrong. He had done what he thought was best, knowing that she wouldn't appreciate it.

Did he always do that with her? With anyone? With his…with his mother?

Yes. He did. It was so clear to him that he could have been staring at its physical form right in front of him. But he didn't want to look at it by himself. He wanted to talk to Alexa. He wanted to share it with her; share everything with her. Because she was his friend, and because he loved her.

He was halfway to her place when he wondered whether it was a good idea. It was the middle of the night on a Saturday. Not to mention the fact that she clearly didn't consider him her friend. She certainly didn't love him. It took the rest of the journey there for him to realise he didn't do a good enough job of fighting for her. She might not love him, but he was sure she cared about him, and maybe they could still be friends. He'd take her friendship if he could have nothing else of her.

Then she opened her front door in her pyjamas. A cotton nightgown that dipped in the valley of her full breasts and caressed her growing stomach. He felt a lot of things in that moment. Protectiveness. Desire. Tenderness. Love. None of it inspired him to think of friendship, and he knew he'd made a mistake.

'I shouldn't have come.'

'You realised this because I opened the door?'

'Yes, actually. What were you thinking, coming to the door like this?'

'Excuse me?'

'You're wearing lingerie.'

'This is not lingerie,' she scoffed. 'It's an old cotton nightgown. My oldest, in fact, because it's the most stretched and none of the others fit me.' She frowned. 'You're one to talk.'

He looked down at his T-shirt and jeans. 'I'm perfectly respectable.'

'Except I can see your biceps and your chest muscles.'

'You can't see my chest muscles.'

'Your T-shirt is tight. I can imagine them.'

'You think I'm dressed inappropriately because of your *imagination*?'

She folded her arms. 'Isn't that what you were doing?'

'I… Well, no. Your breasts are right there.'

She looked down, as if seeing them for the first time. 'Oh. I guess this is not only stretchy around my waist.' She shrugged. 'It's not like you haven't seen this much of them before.'

He closed his eyes and prayed for patience. And maybe a douse of cold water. Maybe an ice bucket, because then he could stuff his heart that was beating with love and amusement for her in it, too.

'Do you want to come in?' she asked when he opened his eyes.

'Yes. No. Yes?' He honestly didn't know. 'I have stuff to say.'

'You don't know where you want to say them?'

'I…think I might get distracted inside.'

'Why?' She leaned against the frame. 'Never mind. It doesn't matter.' Folded her arms. 'Say the stuff.'

'You were right,' he blurted out, because he was avoiding her chest and her eyes and because it was bubbling up inside. 'I take responsibility when I don't have to. But I've been doing it my whole life. With my mom, I mean. She needed me, so I don't know if I didn't have to—'

'You didn't,' she interrupted. 'You chose to. Because she's your mother and you love her, and the way that you show you care is by helping. Doing. Protecting.'

He frowned. Her lips curved.

'Maybe I have some stuff to say, too. But please, continue.'

'Very gracious of you.' He cleared his throat. Tried to remember where he was. 'I blamed myself. For her being sick. I had no reason to. She never made me feel that way. But in my kid brain I thought that if I hadn't been there, hadn't been born, she wouldn't have got sick and—'

She'd moved forward, so when he stopped because of the pain, because he needed to, she took his hands. Slowly, she put them on the base of her waist. Cupped his face.

'Just look at me,' she said. 'Look at me and tell me what you need to say.'

She must have woven a spell on him because he said, 'I don't know why I blamed myself. Maybe because my father said we could make things easier for her. If we could make it easier, we could make it harder. Maybe I already had made it harder. Maybe I was the cause of it?'

'Oh, Ben,' she whispered, lowering her hands to his chest. 'She got sick when you were too young to understand it. Of course your father telling you to help her made you think you needed to because you contributed to it.'

'"Maybe", not "of course",' he replied, though he appreciated the understanding. 'But it happened. The responsibility of caring for her was heavy, but I got stronger. Too strong. I carried it even when she didn't want me to. She might not have wanted me to carry it at all.' He shrugged. 'I did the same with you.'

She sucked in her cheeks, releasing it before her mouth fully became a pout.

'Remember earlier, when I said I have some things to say, too?'

'You mean a few minutes ago? Yeah.'

She'd begun to walk her fingers up his chest. At his comment, she paused to pinch him.

'Okay, okay,' he said with a small laugh. 'No more wise-guy comments.'

'Good, because I need to be serious for a moment.' She took a breath. 'You need to learn how to balance it. Caring for someone, and protecting them so blindly that you do silly, unnecessary things.'

'I know. Lex—'

'Shh,' she said, putting a finger on his lips. 'I'm not done yet.'

He nodded for her to continue.

'I need to learn how to not push you away because I'm scared.' She knitted her brows. 'It might be easier for me because I'm tired of doing it. Protecting myself... It's so much work. It takes so much energy to keep up the shield and to be careful.' She leaned her head against his chest. 'And I'm tired of doing that and of being pregnant.' She lifted her head. 'Do you know how tiring it is to be pregnant? I still have five months to go. I can't do it all.'

He bit his lip to keep from laughing.

'Yeah, okay, laugh at the pregnant lady.'

'I'm not laughing at you,' he said, catching her hand and pressing it to his lips. 'I'm happy. It sounds like you're telling me you want me to do the protecting for you.'

'Did you hear nothing of what I just said?'

'Yeah, but I'm still me. I'm still going to want to protect you. But I'm going to try,' he said sincerely. 'It's not healthy. I know that. I know the situation at home with my family isn't healthy, too. It's...it's safe.'

'For them,' she said gently. 'For you, it's familiar. But it's hard. And every time you see your mother in pain, you'll think it's because of you.'

'I can't snap my fingers and have it disappear.'

'I know that. I'm not asking you to. But I am telling you to be intentional. If you want to be happy, you need to move away from safe. You need to stop taking responsibility for people and things that don't need you to do that for them. Or that, quite simply, aren't your responsibility.' She ran her hands up and down his arms. 'Your mother's illness isn't your fault. Nor is my pregnancy. Or my problems.'

He inhaled, then exhaled. Again, when the first time he did made him feel lighter. He hadn't realised until that night how much he'd blamed himself for a range of things. This conversation made him think that he'd gone along with Alexa's plan because he'd blamed himself in some way for how Lee had treated her. He wanted to make up for it, though he couldn't possibly do that when he wasn't the cause of the treatment.

He saw it now. And, as he told Alexa, it wouldn't immediately go away. Especially not with his mother, where things were more complicated. But he promised her he'd try, so he would.

'Does this mean you're not pushing me away any more?'

'What do you think?'

He smiled when she bumped her belly lightly against him, reminding him of how close they were.

'I need you to say it.'

She rolled her eyes. 'You're annoying.'

'But you love me.'

She hesitated, but her eyes were fierce and sure when she nodded. 'I do.'

Who knew such simple words could set off such intense emotion in him?

'I love you, too,' he said softly.

'I know. You've loved me from the day you first saw me.'

'An exaggeration, I think.'

'I could see it in the way you looked at me. You were such a sucker.'

They were still debating when she led him into her flat. Smiling, he closed the door.

EPILOGUE

Four years later

'DO YOU KNOW what's worse than having twin toddlers?'

Benjamin didn't look over, too busy trying to get Tori, his daughter, off her brother. 'Tori, come on. You know you're bigger than Tavier.'

'Don't you dare get off your brother because you feel sorry for him,' Alexa said, kneeling on the sofa and looking over its back at them. 'He needs to learn.'

'You're encouraging this?' Benjamin asked.

'He loves it.'

Tavier gave a giggle just then. Benjamin threw up his hands. 'Honestly. I was trying to help you.'

Tavier grinned, and pulled his sister's hair. She responded by sitting on him. All things considered, they were playing fair.

'You haven't answered my question.'

He went to join her on the sofa. 'I'm too tired to pretend to remember what you asked.'

'What's worse than having twin toddlers?'

'Is this a riddle?'

He pulled her against him. Because she'd been kneeling, she had no way of resisting. Not that she would have resisted, he knew. Their marriage was a lot of debating, teasing—she was still talking about how he'd never found her handkerchief in his room—but none of it had to do with touching.

'It's not a riddle,' she said.

'A puzzle, then?'

'Same thing.'

'I don't think so.'

'Ben,' she said, taking his face in her hands. She did it whenever she was being serious with him. After four years together, two of them in marriage, it had happened all of four times. So he knew she was serious.

'What's worse than twin toddlers?' he repeated.

'I'm not sure. Our restaurants failing.'

'Our restaurants aren't failing.'

Of course they weren't, but he'd needed to say it because he needed to get over that fear. It was still there, though he'd been running In the Rough for three years now. It was still competing with Infinity, but somehow that competition didn't matter, since they were both doing what they loved. They both seemed to be good at it, too.

Of course they weren't failing.

'I give up.'

'So easily.'

'Baby.'

'Fine. What's worse than twin toddlers…is another baby.'

He blinked. 'I'm not sure I follow.'

'I'm pregnant, dummy.'

'You're…' He trailed off. Looked at the twins. 'But they're only three.'

'They'll be four when the baby gets here.'

'You're sure?'

'I'm pretty good at maths,' she said, rolling her eyes.

Now he rolled his. 'No. I meant, are you sure you're pregnant?'

'Doctor's results came back this morning.'

Because he had no words, he drew her in, holding her so damn tightly. Their lives together had been tough. Their family situations weren't easy. His father had passed away round about the same time he'd got the restaurant, but his mother had refused to live with him and Alexa. She'd found herself an assisted care facility, visited them occasionally, and Benjamin had had a tough time accepting that. Alexa had, a year after Lee had promised not to contact her, agreed to see him. It had taken them a lot of work to get to where they were now: Lee's monthly visits.

But all of that had been okay because they'd

had one another. Their family, their kids… It was a life he'd never imagined. It was better than anything Alexa had imagined, she'd told him one night after the twins were born and they were staring at them.

'I can't believe they're yours.'

'Ours,' Alexa had replied, gripping his hand. 'You were here through everything, and you know you love them as much as I do. They're ours.'

She'd changed his life. And now she was doing it again.

'You're the best thing that ever happened to me,' he whispered.

'Wait until we're outnumbered before you say that.'

But she was smiling when he pulled away.

'We're having another baby,' he said.

'We are.' She leaned forward and kissed him. 'I love you.'

'I love you.'

A vase crashed as the twins rolled against the table. He and Alexa both jumped up, but the vase had been on the kitchen table, and the twins had knocked the coffee table, which had then knocked the vase to the ground in the kitchen, away from them. Their children were unharmed. The vase? Not so much. Tori and Tavier stared at them with wide eyes.

'I guess this means they love us, too,' Alexa said when they each had a twin in their arms.

'What a life.'

'What a life,' she repeated, and kissed him again.

* * * * *

If you enjoyed this story,
check out these other great reads
from Therese Beharrie

Island Fling with the Tycoon
From Heiress to Mom
Second Chance with Her Billionaire
Her Festive Flirtation

All available now!